Helen's Orphans

A Novel By

Ron Fritsch

Published by Asymmetric Worlds

For information, address:

Asymmetric Worlds
1657 West Winona Street
Chicago, IL 60640-2707

Front cover art: *Helen of Troy* by Dante Gabriel Rossetti (1863)

For David, Lee Ann and my family

The Characters

Ithaca, Mycenae, Phthia, Salamis and Sparta were ancient Greek kingdoms

Achilles: king of Phthia, Patroclus's companion

Agamemnon: king of Mycenae, Clytemnestra's husband, Orestes's father, Menelaus's brother

Ajax: king of Salamis

Atreus: a former king of Sparta and Mycenae, Menelaus and Agamemnon's father

Clytemnestra: queen of Mycenae, Agamemnon's wife, Orestes's mother, Helen's sister

Hector: a prince of Troy, Priam and Hecuba's older son, Paris's brother

Hecuba: queen of Troy, Priam's wife, Paris and Hector's mother

Helen: queen of Sparta, Menelaus's wife, Hermione's mother, Clytemnestra's sister

Hermione: princess of Sparta, Menelaus and Helen's daughter

Leda: an orphanage guardian who befriends Helen and Clytemnestra in their youth

Lukas: an orphan, Timon's companion, Nestor's nephew

Menelaus: king of Sparta, Helen's husband, Hermione's father, Agamemnon's brother

Nestor: a shepherd, Lukas's uncle

Odysseus: king of Ithaca, Penelope's husband

Orestes: prince of Mycenae, Agamemnon and Clytemnestra's son

Paris: a prince of Troy, Priam and Hecuba's younger son, Hector's brother

Patroclus: Achilles's companion

Penelope: queen of Ithaca, Odysseus's wife

Priam: king of Troy, Hecuba's husband, Paris and Hector's father

Timon: an orphan, Lukas's companion

Chapter One

Timon

Helen, the queen of Sparta, often came to visit the orphanage I grew up in. She sometimes brought the king, Menelaus, and the princess, Hermione, with her.

After all, she liked to tell the orphans, she'd spent her childhood in the same orphanage.

"They found me and my sister in a basket," she'd say, "just outside the front gate."

Everybody knew the story. When the orphanage guardians discovered the basket, Helen was a newborn. The other child in the basket, who they assumed was her sister, was a year older. Her name, sewn into her tunic like Helen's, was Clytemnestra. Their birth dates were embroidered next to their names.

That was only the beginning of Helen's story. Eighteen years later, the kings of Greece decided she was the most beautiful woman in the world. Early in the morning of the day she was to marry one of them, Menelaus, the eighteen-year-old king of Sparta, she left in a ship with a wedding guest, Paris, also eighteen years old, a Trojan prince. The ship was bound for Troy.

The children in the orphanage, to say nothing of the guardians, couldn't put aside the questions all Greeks asked regarding Helen. Had Paris forcibly taken her with him? Or had she run off with him of her own free will?

Whether Helen's leave-taking was an abduction, the official story, or an elopement, as many believed, it precipitated the devastating war the Greek kingdoms fought against Troy. Parents of almost all of the children in the orphanage died in the war.

Helen

During our days on the ship sailing to Troy, the three guards Paris had taken with him to Sparta were somber, as if they anticipated nothing good would come from what Paris and I were doing. They were the same age as us, but they often seemed to me older than they were.

They'd initially assumed Paris and I would share a room on the ship, but he informed them I'd have one of my own.

"We aren't married," I heard him say to them. "Not yet at least."

Helen

On the morning of our arrival in the harbor at Troy, Paris sent one of his guards to the palace. When the guard returned to the ship, he told Paris and me Prince Hector, who was Paris's twenty-two-year-old brother, had agreed to speak with us in his chamber.

Paris and I seated ourselves on chairs facing his brother, who sat on his chair with his feet planted on the floor in front of him and his broad shoulders pulled back as if he'd already inherited his father Priam's throne and was hearing pleas from his subjects. Hector's eyes and hair were the same olive brown as his younger brother's. Their skin was the color of bronze.

Trojan boys and men had chosen to do what the Greeks did then. As if they didn't want to leave their boyhoods behind them, they began shaving off their facial hair as soon as it sprouted. Hector and Paris were no exceptions.

"I understand," Hector said to me, "you're not royalty."

"I grew up in an orphanage," I said. "Nobody knows who my mother and father were."

"And yet," Hector said, "you were betrothed to King Menelaus of Sparta."

"I was."

"I also understand you left Sparta with my brother the morning of the day you were supposed to marry Menelaus."

"I did."

"Achilles, Odysseus, Ajax, Agamemnon and all the other Greek kings were present for your wedding?"

"They were."

"You decided, nevertheless, at the last moment, not to marry Menelaus?"

"As you can see, I sailed to Troy with your brother."

Hector turned to Paris. "They'll demand we send her back to Sparta."

Paris nodded. "I'm certain they will."

2

Helen's Orphans

Hector turned to me. "My brother's guard told me the Greek kings consider you the most beautiful woman in the world."

I shook my head. "That was idle talk. I hope there's a lot more to me than my outward appearance."

Hector nodded. "I'm certain you're right about that. Paris is also more than the winning athlete the Trojan people celebrate and love. And that's why I'm confused. If the Greek kings demand we send you back to Sparta, will you want us to comply?"

"No, I wish to stay here with Paris."

Hector turned to Paris. "Do you want a war with Greece?"

"Absolutely not," Paris replied.

Hector turned to me. "Do you?"

"No," I replied. "But am I supposed to believe two great peoples would fight a war over whose bed an orphan shares? I'm certain Menelaus was in love with me, but I'm just as certain he'll find happiness without me at his side. I'm also confident he'll be a successful king. The Spartan people will come to cherish his fairness. He'll always put their well-being above his own. And of all the Greek kings, he's the one who most wants peace with your people."

Hector blinked his eyes. "But you wish to remain in Troy?"

"Yes."

"You won't go back to Sparta voluntarily?"

"No."

"If the Greek kings declare war on us, they'll need to sail here to fight us. You've already seen the great walls of Troy."

"I was most impressed when I saw them."

They were as high as the tallest trees in Greece. They consisted of rectangular stone blocks laid and mortared together as if they were bricks. Massively wide at their bottom, they narrowed as they rose but still seemed impenetrably thick at their top. Tall watchtowers rose over every entrance to the city like guardian giants from some other world.

"The Greeks will never breach or climb over those walls," Hector said. "And we can hold out here for a long time."

"You make me think," I said, "you're willing to fight a war with the Greeks."

"A defensive war, yes."

"Do you *want* to fight a defensive war with the Greeks?"

3

"Yes, I do," Hector replied. "Some Greeks have chosen to hate Trojans. They fear our rising power and influence in the world. I understand their leader is Agamemnon, the brother of the person you were supposed to marry."

I chose to remain silent.

"A war," Hector said, "can't stop those Greeks from hating Trojans. It can, though, make them respect us and not wish to fight another war with us."

Again, I said nothing.

"My father and mother," Hector said, "won't send you back to Sparta against your will."

Paris and I looked at one another.

We could only hope Achilles, Odysseus, Ajax and the other Greek kings would choose reason over emotion and remain opposed to the war Hector and Agamemnon wanted to fight.

Timon

When I was still quite young, I noticed a difference between the other orphans and me. They all had a connection to the world outside the orphanage. For some of them it was merely a location, a place in Sparta where they'd been born. Others knew the names of their parents and how they'd died. Some even had relatives they could hope to see one day.

Presumably, my father and mother died in the war, but nobody could say for certain they had. Nobody could tell me what their names were, where they'd lived or who their and my relatives might be. I had only my name and my birth date, sewn into my tunic like Helen's and her sister's. Even where that information had come from was a question nobody could answer.

Helen

A messenger from Agamemnon arrived on a Greek merchant ship. Two of the warriors who patrolled the harbor brought the emissary to Hector.

She told him the kings of Greece had met the day I was supposed to marry Menelaus, who chose not to speak. Agamemnon made his

4

younger brother's case for him. Achilles, Odysseus, Ajax and the other Greek kings agreed with Agamemnon this time. The Trojans would either return me to Sparta on the ship with the messenger, or they'd be at war with all the Greek armies under Agamemnon's command.

Hector asked the messenger to inform Agamemnon, and through him the other Greek kings, his father and mother wouldn't order my return to Sparta. I wished to remain in Troy, and my hosts would grant my request not to be removed from the people I'd chosen to live with.

The messenger asked Hector why the Greeks should believe that was my choice.

Because, Hector told the messenger, he said it was. And if the Greeks in fact started a war over such a trivial matter, they might begin to wonder if their reputation as a great people was no longer justified. Or were they simply using an orphan's presence in Troy as an excuse to attack a people who sought nothing more than the enjoyment of equal status with their neighbors?

Helen

After the messenger left, the Trojans removed their ships from their harbor, choosing not to fight what Hector told Paris and me would be a losing naval battle with the invading Greeks.

"They have too many ships," Hector said, as we viewed the harbor-clearing activity from the top of the watchtower above the main entrance to Troy, "and we have too few."

He was adamant, though, he could defeat the Greeks by keeping them out of Troy for however long they'd be willing to attempt to break into it.

I told Paris and Hector I'd never wish to kill or injure a fellow Greek, but I'd consider it an honor to help the Trojans defend their city. As the other persons in Troy who could do so did, I spent every day, usually next to Paris, doing what had to be done before the Greeks arrived.

The main task was bringing into the city all the farmers and their moveable property, including their livestock and grain supplies. The countryside Trojan farmers occupied extended to the north, east and south of the city. After that was done, Paris and I helped block the entrances to the city, piling up the timbers and boulders the Trojans had used for that purpose on previous occasions.

5

Unusual storms swept the sea between Greece and Troy, giving the Trojans more time to prepare than they'd anticipated they'd have. But eventually the Greeks filled the harbor with their ships. I doubted they numbered as many as some observers chose to say later, but there were far more of them than even the most pessimistic Trojans had expected.

So many ships, so many sailors, so many warriors, I thought, and all because Paris had abducted me, or I'd decided to run off to Troy with him. The Greeks and their kings had become victims of Agamemnon's madness. I couldn't imagine sensible people would ever go to war over a broken promise to marry, no matter who the aggrieved person was.

Timon

Whether Paris had abducted Helen or she'd gone with him to Troy voluntarily, after the Trojan War ended, Menelaus married her and made her the queen of Sparta.

On the day of their marriage, he placed her in charge of the orphanage. On that same day, she promised the people of Sparta she'd make certain the guardians of the orphanage treated each and every orphan kindly and well. Most of the children she was now responsible for, she pointed out, had lost at least one parent in the war. But all of them, she said, deserved the very best upbringing and education Sparta had to offer.

She kept her promise. We spent part of every day receiving instructions in reading, writing, mathematics, chemistry, biology, botany, astronomy, history, geography, poetry, singing, dancing, playing musical instruments and competing in athletic games.

We spent part of every day working, too. Working itself wasn't optional, but where and how we spent our time working were. The guardians expected very young children to do little more than wash themselves and their clothes and air the blankets they slept on and under.

By the time we reached our sixth birthday, the guardians encouraged us to spend parts of our days working on other things. Adhering to Helen's kindness rule, the guardians couldn't require how much time we worked or how much effort we put into what we did. They could only ask us to please do something worthwhile. A few of the orphans took that to mean they could do anything more than nothing and get by. Most of us, though, sooner or later saw the work requirement, as Helen

Helen's Orphans

told us she did—as a way to learn how to do a job we could get paid for doing when we turned eighteen and left the orphanage.

Another boy who was my age, Lukas, had become my friend. With our dark brown hair and eyes, we resembled one another so much we could've passed for brothers. He and I, always side by side like a pair of young oxen, tried our hands at a number of things.

We discovered why so many orphans chose to work in the kitchen. Some took turns distracting the guardians while their accomplices sampled the food without getting caught. Lukas and I decided we could wait for the regular meal periods to taste the food.

We saw why others fell in love with the horses and enjoyed nothing more than feeding and grooming them in their stable. They insisted, as often as they could, the steeds needed to pull chariots for exercise. And who else but their caregivers, they asked, should drive the chariots?

We tried other things. We worked in the vegetable garden for a while, and in the fruit orchard and the vineyard as well. We herded sheep and goats in the hills. We tended the ducks and geese at their ponds. We sowed, harvested and milled wheat and barley.

We ultimately chose, though, to work in the olive grove. The older girl and boy who managed it, and were lovers, had already been promised jobs in the largest olive grove in Sparta. In the brief time before they planned to leave the orphanage and marry, they taught us how to prune the trees and carve the cuttings into bowls and ladles for the kitchen and dining room. We also learned from them how to process the olives we harvested, soaking in brine those intended for the table and pressing the others for their oil.

They were all laborious, time-consuming tasks, but Lukas and I enjoyed hard work. We especially liked to see what it was doing to our growing bodies.

Ron Fritsch

Chapter Two

Helen

The Greek kings could've gotten by with far fewer ships if they'd sent only their warriors to destroy Troy. But they'd forced civilians, both men and women, into their armies as well.

"We want the fittest in the land," they'd told the warriors they sent to find the recruits.

Heroes didn't do the day-to-day work of besieging a magnificent walled city. Shepherds, with arrows aimed at their backs when the occasion arose, took on a large share of those tasks. Many of them, I suspected, had previously confronted nothing more threatening than angry ewes and nannies protecting their lambs and kids from what they perceived as mistreatment.

Clutching a body shield with one hand and a hook attached to a battering ram with the other, those contributing to the war effort against their will ran toward the blocked-up entrances to Troy. After the ram crashed against the tightly packed timbers and boulders, the battering teams backed up, caught their breath, and brought their rams forward again.

Inside the walls, those of us guarding the entrances piled even more timbers and boulders, from Hector's ample supply of them, wherever we decided there was even a slight possibility a ram might eventually break through. Hector encouraged us to take no chances.

The ramming continued, day after day. Despite their shields, some of the Greeks doing the tedious work suffered injuries, many of them fatal. Paris and the other most skilled archers in Troy peered down from the watchtowers, waiting for a worker's misstep. The Trojans had spent days plowing furrows into the ground crosswise to the routes they knew the Greeks bearing battering rams would need to take.

Whenever the shield of a member of a ramming gang shifted enough to reveal part of the head, chest or belly of the worker, a Trojan archer would fire an arrow and often stop the crew until the wounded—and usually dying—conscript was removed and a replacement brought in.

The Greek archers on the ground posed little danger to their Trojan counterparts, who fought in high watchtower positions behind holes in the walls only large enough for one archer to view the terrain below and aim and fire arrows.

The Greeks gave their archers a different task to perform. Day and night, at unpredictable times and places, they fired flaming arrows over the walls. Although the great height of the walls caused the arrows to fall a short distance inside the city, they often landed where many Trojans needed to be—near the entrances, making certain they remained blocked up.

The Trojan children turned the Greeks' flaming arrows into a game, seeking to be the first to spot one and shout "Arrow!" to anybody who happened to be in the area where it would come tumbling down. Then the group of youngsters that child was with would run to the fallen arrow with containers of water and blankets and quickly put out the fire. But the children would grow tired of the game every day, and adults would have to replace them, keeping their eyes on the sky, their containers filled with water, and their blankets in hand.

The Greek archers each had three comrades who held shields in front of them and lit their arrows. The archers needed to carefully time what they did. If they shot their arrows too soon, the flame would go out. If they shot their arrows too late, their bows would catch fire and burn their hands. Sometimes in the excitement of their work a comrade would let a shield slip, and a watchful Trojan archer would take a shot and wound a member of their party. More than a few of those injured had Paris to blame for their agonizing deaths.

Hector was jubilant. Neither the battering rams nor the flaming arrows, he said, would bring about the destruction of Troy. He told Paris and me he was damned glad we'd lured the Greeks to Troy to fetch me and take me home—and attempt to destroy a walled city as they did so. We'd enticed them into the blood-splattered trap he'd set for them.

Helen

I sometimes climbed the stairs to the main-entrance watchtower Paris occupied to shoot his arrows. Once, to see as much as I could, like a child unable to restrain her curiosity, I leaned over the top of the wall too far and for too long, and a Greek archer fired an arrow at me. I ducked down in time to avoid taking a hit, but I could still hear the arrow whizzing by not far above my head.

Like many Greeks at that time, the archer who'd shot at me probably believed I was a traitor. She might've assumed, if she'd killed me, she'd be celebrated forever as the warrior who'd taken down Helen herself high on a wall at Troy.

Her near miss, though, was fortuitous for me. When Menelaus heard about it, he prevailed upon his brother Agamemnon to issue a special order to all the Greek armies. No one should make any attempt to harm me. Menelaus had reminded Agamemnon my return to Greece was the reason they were at war with the Trojans. From the day I'd left Sparta with Paris, Agamemnon had insisted I was an innocent victim and not a lovesick traitor. He'd wanted to cast in the worst possible light the cruel Trojan prince who'd forced me to go with him to Troy.

"That's what the uncivilized Trojans do," he'd say. "They steal whatever they want."

Sometimes, though, when Agamemnon wasn't within earshot, his wife Clytemnestra told people she wouldn't be surprised if her sister had talked Paris into taking her back to Troy with him. Helen, she confided, was an attention-seeking, live-for-the-moment person who'd have no qualms about doing that. Clytemnestra knew nobody would dare repeat those remarks to Agamemnon—and appear to question, to his face, the honesty of the great king.

Timon

Lukas and I weren't very old when we discovered how much we liked music. Whenever we were alone, working or playing, we sang together.

The guardians who taught music at the orphanage took note of what we'd accomplished on our own and granted our request for individual instruction. They taught us how to play the lyre and the pan flute and accompany one another singing.

Then hair grew on our bodies. We tolerated it in our armpits and pubic regions. But, like the other Greek boys and men of that era, as if we were jealous of girls and women with their hairless faces, we shaved every bristle off our cheeks and chins every morning.

Our voices changed too. Lukas became a tenor, and I a baritone. He could still reach some of the higher notes boys and women had no trouble singing. I, though, despite my best efforts, could not. I learned instead to increase the volume of my voice. One instructor told me she wanted it to sound, at its deepest and darkest, like rolling thunder in a storm.

Our instructors began to request we perform for the other orphans and guardians. We insisted, though, we only wanted to entertain ourselves in the olive grove. Our instructors told us we were selfish. They said people with skills like ours, whether we were born with them or had developed them through tedious practice, should wish to share what we could do.

"That's what kind and generous people do," one instructor told us.

I'd already guessed they had something else in mind for us, but I chose not to discuss it then with Lukas.

Helen

Early one morning the Greeks sent a messenger from their harbor encampment across the treeless plain toward the city. She held an olive branch above her head as if it were a torch lighting her way. When she came within shouting distance of the watchtower above the main entrance to the city, she disclosed the purpose of her visit.

"I have a message for Paris," she said, "from King Menelaus of Sparta."

Paris and I had already reached his usual position above the main entrance. Noting that the Greek archers were well beyond their firing range, as were the other Greek warriors, he revealed himself at the top of the wall to the messenger.

"What's the message from King Menelaus?" he asked.

"King Menelaus challenges you to a duel with spears and swords," the messenger replied. "The loser will die. The winner will have Helen to do with as he pleases."

"This is outrageous," I said to Paris. "This challenge isn't from Menelaus."

The messenger had more information for Paris and the Trojans. "When the duel ends with the death of one of you," she said, "this war will end. Helen will either go home to Sparta or remain here. In either case, the Greek armies will go home."

I turned to Paris again. "This challenge is from Agamemnon, and he's lying. No matter how your combat with Menelaus ends, the Greek armies won't go home, and the war won't end. Why should you risk your life in such a useless duel?"

Paris shrugged. "Why should Menelaus risk his life in such a useless duel?"

"He shouldn't," I said. "Agamemnon has forced him to do it. You know that."

Paris stared at the Greek armies. "I don't doubt what you say is true. But the other Greeks out there don't know Agamemnon will renege on his promise to end the war. And my fellow Trojans don't know it either. Both sides surely want to believe the end of this war will only require the death of Menelaus or me. Menelaus has to fight me for the Greeks. I have to fight him for the Trojans."

I shook my head. "To hell with my simple-minded Greeks. To hell with your simple-minded Trojans too. I don't want to see either you or Menelaus dead. Least of all do I want to see one of you kill the other."

Paris and I could hear Hector making his way up the stairs to the watchtower.

When he reached us, he looked at Paris. "You have to fight Menelaus."

I was incredulous. "You want your brother to risk his life in a useless duel?"

Hector looked at me. "Why will this duel be useless?"

"You should know Agamemnon by now as well as I do. He'll never keep his promise to end the war no matter what happens in any damned duel. Doesn't that make it useless?"

Hector shook his head. "Not at all. If Agamemnon reneges on his promise to end the war, all the world will know him forever for the war-loving liar he is. If Menelaus and Paris fight the duel, and one of them wins, and one of them dies, and the war goes on, both your Greeks and my Trojans will know this war has never been fought over you. We Trojans will know Agamemnon began his attack on our city because he hates us. And we'll fight his war to the death of us all if we have to. Sooner, rather than later, your Greeks will see that. They'll force

Agamemnon to give up his hopeless attempt to destroy our city. They'll load up their ships and go home."

Paris addressed the messenger as well as the Greek armies in the distance. "The duel will begin at noon. The Greek armies will remain where they are now. My fellow Trojans will venture no farther from the city walls than the Greeks are from the harbor. Menelaus and I, and only he and I, will be present for our duel at the midway point between the harbor and the city. We'll both bring a spear and a sword to fight with and water and wine to drink."

The messenger turned to Menelaus, who nodded in agreement with the rules Paris had offered him.

Helen

Hector and I chose to view the duel from the watchtower above the main entrance.

Menelaus and Paris first thrust at one another with their spears, then slashed with their swords. Neither could land a blow on the other's body. They continued, though, often coming close enough to an insertion of a point of a spear into the other's belly or a tip of a sword across the other's throat to cause the onlookers on both sides to swoon.

And so the duel to the death of one of them, and the victory of the other—who'd supposedly win the possession of me, to do with as he pleased—went on throughout the afternoon. The combatants provided their partisans with enough footwork and thrusting of spears and slashing of swords for at least ten such duels. They came so close to killing the other so many times the admiring crowds paid no attention to the passage of the day.

I could see Menelaus and Paris were using their nimble athletic abilities to make it look as if their opponent's skillful evasions, and not their own reluctance to kill the other, kept them from landing a harmful, let alone fatal, blow. They carried on in that manner until sunset, depriving the spectators, Greeks and Trojans alike, of their supper at the usual time for it.

As the sun slipped below the sea beyond the harbor, Paris threw down his weapon, which was then his spear, and refused to pick up his sword.

Helen's Orphans

"I can't defeat you, Menelaus," he said. "I refuse to shame myself by making any further attempt to do what I know I can't do."

Menelaus also threw down his spear and chose not to pick up his sword.

"Nor can I defeat you, Paris," he said. "The shame would be mine if I tried again."

The war would go on, and I'd remain no man's possession, to do with as he pleased.

Helen

"You think," Hector asked me in the watchtower, "if Paris had killed Menelaus, Agamemnon would've continued the war?"

"He would've found some reason to do it. I suspect he would've accused Paris of cheating somehow. But if Menelaus had killed Paris, what would you've done?"

Hector turned to me. "That decision would've been yours. If you'd wanted to go back to Sparta, I would've let you go. I would've preferred, though, you chose to stay here. I could've claimed you and I had never agreed to the terms of the duel."

And if I'd chosen to remain in Troy, the war would've gone on.

Agamemnon had forced Menelaus into the duel only because Achilles, Odysseus and Ajax had insisted upon one. Their shepherds clutching their battering rams were dying. Their archers were wasting their arrows and, some of them, their lives. And the heroes could no longer imagine a war with no end in sight would bring them any opportunity for glory for themselves.

But they weren't disappointed the duel hadn't ended the fighting. It changed their minds instead. They wanted the war to go on. Menelaus and Paris, who'd fought their deadly duel to a draw, were the heroes of the war at that point.

Achilles, Odysseus and Ajax hadn't seen the cleverly feigned duel I saw. No, after the duel, they wanted the siege of Troy to continue to its end, however long it took. Only then could they hope to become the greatest hero of the war, the warrior who killed Hector. They'd seen him on top of the watchtower with me.

But I didn't give a damn whether Menelaus and Paris were heroes or not. What mattered to me was, they'd expertly kept each other alive—

and fooled the people, Greeks as well as Trojans, into thinking they'd fought a duel to the death. A duel they both walked away from without suffering the loss of a single drop of their blood.

I hadn't anticipated Hector's next remark. "I'm as glad as you are they faked it."

Chapter Three

Timon

Lukas and I sang for the other orphans and the guardians at the next holiday, this one celebrating the end of winter and the beginning of spring.

We were seventeen years old then. Lukas had grown taller than me by half the length of our middle fingers. Our work in the olive grove had made us both as muscular as we'd hoped, growing up, we'd become. When we wrestled, only rarely could one of us pin the other. Almost every match ended in our mutual exhaustion. Our inability to win, though, didn't keep us from looking forward to our next head-to-toe encounter with the other's writhing, sweat-covered body.

We sang the lyrics and ballads our people traditionally sang. When fools and charlatans got—or didn't get—what they deserved, our audience laughed. When lovers broke through—or failed to break through—the barriers keeping them apart, our listeners wept tears of joy or sorrow, or they at least had to struggle not to.

Our instructors told us afterward we'd have to perform again.

"Why don't you sing," one instructor asked, "the next time Helen pays us a visit?"

That was what I'd guessed the instructors had in mind for Lukas and me all along.

Timon

"I'll never sing for Helen," Lukas told me when we were alone again in the olive grove.

The preceding winter had been lethal for one of our oldest trees. We'd finished removing it the day before, and the time had come to plant a sapling we'd grown, from a domesticated stem we'd grafted onto a wild root, to take the dead tree's place.

"You won't sing for our benevolent queen?" I asked.

Lukas scoffed. "Not for the benevolent queen who ran off with a Trojan prince and started a horrible war that killed my mother and father. What makes you think I'd want to sing for the person who did that?"

Warriors had come for Lukas's parents and uncle, who were shepherds, and compelled them, at spearpoint, to go to Troy to assist in fighting the enemy.

I shrugged. "Maybe Helen didn't willingly run off to Troy with Paris. Some people truly believe he abducted her and gave her no choice. That's what the guardians say."

Lukas shook his head. "They would say that, but my uncle says it isn't the truth."

The uncle, Nestor, was a year younger than his brother, Lukas's father. Unlike Lukas's parents, Nestor had survived the war. He'd come home from it, though, without his left foot.

Lukas was ten years old when Nestor managed to make his only trip to see his nephew. A neighbor who came to the orphanage to see a niece had given Nestor a ride in her carriage.

"You remember," Lukas asked, "what he told us about Helen?"

I nodded. Nestor had said he knew for a fact Helen had run off to Troy voluntarily. When Lukas asked him how he knew that, he declined to say. He told us he didn't want to talk about it then. Maybe someday, when we were older, he'd tell us.

"Even if your uncle is right," I said, "Helen might not have believed running off with Paris would start a war."

Lukas shook his head again. "She had to have known a war was a possibility. She'd promised a Greek king she'd marry him. She chose instead to sail across the sea with a Trojan prince. I suspect she simply didn't give a damn if she started a war that left me and a bunch of other kids orphans. And you want me to sing for her?"

I resumed gently shoveling earth over the roots of our sapling. I couldn't stop thinking, though, our refusal to sing for Helen would be a mistake.

"She's our benefactor," I said. "She's been very good to everybody in this orphanage. You've heard the guardians say how much she's improved things here. I have no reason to doubt they're telling us the truth about that."

I finished my work and turned to Lukas. He was staring at our sapling and pouting the way he sometimes did to turn me on and give him what he wanted. I had to ignore that for a moment and continue my argument.

18

Helen's Orphans

"Maybe," I said, "Helen did choose to do what you accuse her of doing. But she was about the same age we are now, not much more than a child. Maybe she regrets what she did. I think whatever youthful mistake Helen might've made years ago, we need to show her our gratitude for what she's done for us and the other orphans. She didn't personally murder your parents. She didn't order the warriors to round up shepherds to help fight the Trojans."

I took Lukas in my arms and kissed him on his lips. I guessed we'd soon have to remove our clothes right there in the olive grove. It was still cool enough to do what we needed to do with the sun on our bodies.

"Please sing with me for Helen," I said. "Please do it for the other orphans. If she didn't look out for us, this place would be the prison they say it used to be. Please do it for them."

Lukas looked at me as if he couldn't decide whether he loathed me or loved me.

"I'll sing with you when Helen comes again," he said. "But I won't do it for her. I'll do it for the orphans."

I pressed my lips against his just in time to taste the tears rolling down his cheeks like raindrops.

He was one of the many Greeks who couldn't forgive Helen for what they believed she'd done to bring on the Trojan War. I was one of the many Greeks who wanted to focus on the person Helen had become, whatever she'd done, or not done, in her youth.

Helen

After the duel in which Menelaus and Paris used their gymnastic skills to simulate fierce attempts to kill the other, with many close calls, the siege of Troy resumed. Within the walls of their city the Trojans had a number of fruit orchards, vineyards, olive and nut groves and vegetable gardens. I worked in all of them, as I had in the orphanage in Sparta.

I realized helping the Trojans grow food would extend the siege and increase the number of Greek warriors and workers Paris and the other Trojan archers would injure and kill. On the other hand, I lived with the Trojans then, and I couldn't sit idle knowing I might someday watch them starve.

Ron Fritsch

Early on in my work, I discovered the Greek and Trojan horticultural methods differed in a number of important ways. The Greek practices I'd learned in the orphanage usually seemed improvements on what the Trojans did. In some cases, though, I had to admit the Trojans produced better yields than my fellow Greeks did.

I didn't anticipate the persons in charge of the orchards, vineyards, groves and gardens would be open to my suggestions for changes in what they did. When I offered them anyway, as if I were imitating my know-it-all sister Clytemnestra, they put up little or no resistance.

That didn't surprise Paris. He'd come to the orchard I was working in to share a midday meal with me. He'd brought a blanket we spread on the ground in the shade of an apple tree.

"Trojans," he said, "are brought up believing Greeks are superior to them in every way imaginable. Your athletes are better. Your ships are bigger and faster. Even your language is lovelier than ours."

Most Trojans, I'd learned, taught their children Greek as well as their own language as soon as they started speaking.

"But Hector," I said, "thinks your Trojans can defeat the Greeks in a war."

"Only in a defensive war," Paris said. "He'd never attempt to fight your Greeks outside the walls of this city."

Timon

Lukas and I sang in front of the terraced slope that served as an amphitheater for the orphanage. Helen sat at the center of the bottom row. Whatever Lukas might've wanted, I suspected the fawning guardians on either side of their generous patron had assured her she was the member of our audience we most wished to please.

We included in our repertoire a song Lukas had insisted we sing. A princess marries a handsome prince against the stern warning of her older sister. Within days of the wedding, the princess finds her new husband in bed with a servant, proving her sister was right.

Helen, who appeared as serene during the song as a lark at sunrise, gave no indication she thought the lyrics applied to her.

Her sister Clytemnestra, though, had insinuated, on more than one occasion during the war, they did. "Who knows what that woman-chasing prince is up to in Troy?" she'd ask. "What could Helen do if she found him in bed with a servant? Complain to the king and queen and Hector? Why would they listen to a word she said? She's nothing but a servant herself."

Timon

At the conclusion of our performance, Helen approached us, even as the guardians and the other orphans continued their generous standing ovation.

"You both have lovely voices," she said. "Your songs brought more tears to my eyes than I could've imagined it was possible for me to shed."

I accepted her embrace.

Lukas stood silent and expressionless.

Helen and I were the same height. So was Menelaus. So, she'd told me once, was Paris. Her golden-brown hair fell in waves past her shoulders. Her loose-fitting tunic couldn't conceal what, according to many accounts, had driven Menelaus and Paris to fight to the death for her.

The intensity of her eyes told her darkest story. She was inside Troy when it fell. She'd seen hundreds of Greeks and Trojans fatally injured and maimed.

I'd spoken with Helen on many previous occasions. The more I had, the more I'd come to doubt she would've willingly boarded a ship bound for Troy if even the thinnest cloud of a possibility of starting a war hovered over it. I couldn't understand why Lukas was so certain of her wrongdoing.

Timon

I was glad, though, he listened to the other orphans and the guardians. They insisted we sing for Helen during her subsequent visits.

"She loves you," many of them told us.

"She takes every request of ours to Menelaus," one of the guardians wasn't above mentioning. "And she somehow convinces him to grant far more of them than any previous king of Sparta ever did."

"I've heard," another guardian said, "she doesn't need to relay our requests to the king. She decides to grant them herself."

Lukas agreed to continue singing.

Helen

I decided the time had come to tell Paris what I wanted to do. "Nobody knows," I said, "how long this damned war will go on." He and I were eating another midday meal together, this one in a grove of fig trees I was working in that day, far from the useless but incessant battering rams and flaming arrows at the walls.

He shrugged. "Not even my brother is willing to speculate about that."

"Meanwhile," I said, "you and I will only grow older."

Paris laid down his spoon and stopped eating his lentil soup and bread.

"Meanwhile, too," I said, wrapping my arm around his narrow waist, "you and I are missing out on the joy love brings lovers."

He stared at me as if he were on the verge of winning yet another of the athletic contests he couldn't get enough of, and the happy crowd, filled with his admirers, was going wild.

"I've made up my mind," I said. "I want to share a bed with you."

It would only take him one more throw, shot, lap or takedown, the look on his face told me, before he'd stand in the winner's circle wearing a laurel wreath again. Like a goddess in an old story, I'd give him this victory.

Then he frowned. "I can only share a bed with you if we're married. My family has strict rules about that sort of thing. I've always promised my mother and father I'd obey those rules."

"I wouldn't want you to violate your family's rules. I'm asking you to marry me."

"You wanted to marry Menelaus."

"I did. I wanted to marry him and share a bed with him. If I were in Sparta, I'd still want to marry him and share a bed with him. But, thanks to this war, I don't think I'll return to Sparta anytime soon. And now I find myself wanting to marry you and share a bed with you. I feel I'm facing reality. I'm here in Troy with you. I'm not in Sparta with Menelaus anymore."

"You're still in love with him, though?"

Helen's Orphans

"I'll always be in love with him. He was the kind and gentle youth who took me from a miserable orphanage to his palace."

"And you also found him pleasing to your eyes."

"I did. He was as pleasing to my eyes as you are. But I'm not eating my lunch in this fig grove with him. I'm with you."

I drew Paris close to me and kissed him on his lips. I reached under his tunic and felt what I knew he had for me there.

He moaned. "My father can marry us."

"Ask him to do it this afternoon. We don't need a celebration with thousands of guests, not in the middle of a war. The people will understand. Tonight will be our wedding night."

"I'll at least find some rose petals to sprinkle on our bed."

I laughed. "I'd love rose petals sprinkled on our bed. I've never done this before, you know."

"Neither have I."

I laughed again. "I don't have the slightest doubt about that."

Ron Fritsch

Chapter Four

Helen

Priam married Paris and me in his chamber. Hecuba and Hector were the only witnesses. With their full heads of gray hair and deeply wrinkled faces, Priam and Hecuba looked as if they were old enough to be the grandparents of Hector and Paris. And, of course, they were that old. Priam's younger brother had taken hostage their first set of children— two boys, fifteen and seventeen, and a girl, sixteen. He threatened to kill them if Priam refused to abdicate in favor of him. Refusing to believe his brother would murder his nephews and niece, Priam chose not to comply with his demand. After the brother carried out his threat and murdered the children, the horrified Trojans rose up and killed the traitor and his supporters. Priam and Hecuba decided to have more children. As a result, Hecuba gave birth to Hector and Paris.

After we'd said the words necessary for a Trojan wedding, Hecuba turned to me.

"I understand," she said, "the king of Sparta was riding in his chariot past the orphanage where you grew up. He saw you, decided you should be his wife and ordered you to go with him to his palace."

That was how the Trojans told my story, as if I'd had no choice in the matter—as if I hadn't, as Clytemnestra liked to put it, shamelessly thrown myself at Menelaus.

"So when this handsome Trojan prince here," Hecuba continued, gesturing toward Paris, "came to attend your wedding, you decided you'd rather run off with him than marry the king of Sparta. And you chose to do your running off the very morning of the day the king had selected for your wedding. That's the kind of comeuppance a haughty king deserves when he tries to force a lovely young woman like yourself into being his bride. When I first heard what you'd done, it made me so happy I burst into tears. I knew right then Paris should marry you."

Paris and I remained silent, as we had to.

"You'd think," Hecuba said, "the king of Sparta and his evil brother Agamemnon would've left the matter there. But no, they decided to start a war just to get you back. Have you ever heard of a more foolish reason for a war?"

Hector scoffed. "Agamemnon used what Helen and Paris did as an excuse to start the war he's always wanted. Our people who trade with the Greeks all tell me that. But rest assured, we'll make Agamemnon and those other Grecian kings regret their decision. They'll go home wishing they'd never heard of the great walled city known as Troy."

Helen

Menelaus found out I'd married Paris the day after I did it. In a quiet moment one of the Trojan archers leaned over the top of the watchtower she was shooting her arrows from and yelled down the news to the Greeks.

Her attempt to taunt the enemy brought an arrow flying toward her from the same archer who'd shot at me. This arrow also missed its target as closely as mine had.

I assumed the Greek warriors and workers who were risking their lives every day must've found the war unbearable by then. They knew, whatever their kings ordered them to do, their risk-taking had no real purpose except to harass the people behind the massive walls until they starved to death. And who could say how long that would take?

Timon

Lukas and I returned from the olive grove one afternoon and sang for our instructors a song we told them we wished to sing the next time we performed for Helen.

We were only three lines into it when they began looking at one another and rolling their eyes. After we finished singing it, they all gave us the same reason for dismissing it—they hadn't heard it before.

"Yeah," Lukas said, "there's a damned good reason you haven't heard it before. Timon and I created the lyrics and music on our own. We'd never heard it before either."

"You know you can't do that," one instructor said. "You know there's no such thing as a new song."

Helen's Orphans

That was their rule. We could only sing songs our ancestors had sung. Our people were so brilliant we'd long ago composed every song worth singing. We had no need for any more.

Lukas scoffed. "You just heard a new song. Wasn't it lovely?"

"It doesn't matter if you think it's lovely or not," the instructor said. "Our people haven't heard it before. It isn't one of our songs. Nobody can sing something like that. It's totally unexpected. It comes from nowhere."

Lukas shook his head. "Timon and I have decided the rule against no new songs is silly. We think songs can be as infinite as the stars in the night sky. We plan to compose more new songs."

The instructor shrugged. "You can waste your time doing that," she said, "but you can't perform your new songs in this orphanage."

"And certainly not," another instructor said, "when Helen, the most generous benefactor we've ever had, comes to hear you."

Lukas and I had known how our instructors would react to our song. But that only meant we'd have to defy them.

Helen

Because I was now a princess, I could have official duties to perform. Hector asked his father to put me in charge of all the orchards, vineyards, groves and gardens in Troy.

My new mother-in-law Hecuba agreed. "I've heard about your horticultural work. I'm so glad my son stole you away from those Greeks. We deserve you more than they do."

Hector looked at me. "If we're going to win this war, we'll need every extra olive, grape, fig, berry and walnut you can bring us."

"I wish to keep your people alive and well," I said.

Priam appointed me the royal gardener of Troy.

Helen

I spent every day from sunrise to sunset in an orchard, vineyard, grove or garden. I worked alongside the other workers, doing whatever they did, wherever they needed extra help planting, pruning, weeding or harvesting. I suspected they went home in the evening and told their families and neighbors they'd worked that day with the orphan Paris had brought home from Sparta.

"They fell in love," I heard someone say.

The speaker didn't know I was on a ladder in a nearby tree picking plums.

"She got on his ship and came to Troy with him," the person said. "Who can blame her? I'd do it myself if Paris asked me to. But I still don't understand why that brought every Greek army to the walls of Troy."

Neither did I. I confess, though, my hatred of the war those Greek armies had brought with them didn't diminish my happiness inside the walls of Troy sharing a life with Paris.

Timon

Helen sat in her usual place, straight ahead of Lukas and me at the center of the lowest terrace. We sang several of the old songs she'd told us she especially enjoyed hearing us sing. The guardians on either side of her applauded and cheered our selections as vigorously and loudly as the most uninhibited orphans did.

Then Lukas began singing a song we'd created. I played the pan flute. He played the lyre.

We ignored the growing anguish of the guardians. We could see the wide-eyed surprise of the orphans. At first, they probably thought it was a song they couldn't remember hearing before.

> *They tended flocks on sunlit pastures.*
> *They had no need for surly masters.*
> *One day they chose to have each other*
> *And vowed they'd never please another.*
> *Then war broke out among mad kings,*
> *Who fought for glory, greed and rings.*
> *The shepherds crossed a storm-tossed sea*
> *And died for nothing, leaving me.*

Lukas sang the last two lines twice more as a chorus.

Helen's Orphans

As the music faded away, a number of the orphans, having realized Lukas was singing about his mother and father, were in tears. The guardians maintained their silence.

The song violated many more rules than the one prohibiting the singing of nontraditional lyrics. Surely Menelaus, the reigning king of Sparta, could be included as one of the mad kings war broke out among. The rings obviously referred to those Helen didn't exchange with Menelaus but did with Paris. The song also put front and center the lives and fates of nonentities, two insignificant shepherds. And it fatally injected the composer-singer into the song. All the guardians cringed when they heard the last word—the unacceptable, unimaginable *me*.

Lukas wasn't singing about far-off heroes and their equally far-off enemies, as he was expected to do. He was singing about people in the here and now—including, most outrageously, himself.

Then Helen stood up and began applauding. The distraught guardians could only stand up themselves, fix smiles of joy on their faces and applaud. The orphans, many of them wiping their eyes, joined their elders in their appreciation for a song coming out of nowhere.

Helen

The Greeks gave up attempting to unblock the entrances to Troy with their battering rams. From the watchtowers the Trojans could see what was happening. The workers the Greek kings had conscripted into their armies were dragging the rams to the harbor and stacking them next to the largest tent in the main encampment of the Greek armies. The Trojans had assumed from the beginning the tent was Agamemnon's.

The Greek archers, though, continued firing flaming arrows over the walls every day and night. They gave Hector no alternative but to keep sky-watchers, as they'd come to be known, on duty at all times. They had to be ready, with their many blankets and containers of water, to pick them up, run as fast as they could and put out another fire. Hector ordered those who fell asleep on duty to help empty the public latrines for the next ten days.

Some of the sky-watchers extinguishing the fires had suffered burns, all but a few of them minor, but no Trojan had died yet as a direct result of the war. The people tended to believe, as I did, Hector was right. They had more than enough stores of grain and other dry food supplies—

29

together with the harvests from their orchards, vineyards, groves and gardens—to keep them and their livestock alive for years to come. Long before they'd begin to starve, the Greeks would surely conclude the siege of Troy was an intolerably expensive folly and go home. I couldn't imagine any humans could hate other humans as much as it would take for them to continue their siege.

Helen

Hector and I paid a visit to the watchtower above the main entrance to Troy. Paris wanted us to see what he'd seen.

He pointed toward the main Greek encampment at the harbor. "Their stack of battering rams is dwindling."

Hector laughed. "That's what you asked us to come here and see?"

Paris wasn't laughing. "Can't you tell," he asked, "they have fewer battering rams piled there than they had before?"

Hector shrugged. "Not really. They had quite a few battering rams to begin with. I'd say they still have quite a few."

Paris shook his head. "But not as many as they had before."

"I know you have good eyes," Hector said, peering at the Greeks' encampment. "You couldn't be the best archer in Troy if you didn't. Suppose I agree with you their pile is less substantial than it was? What difference does it make?"

"Ask yourself a question," Paris said. "What are the Greeks doing with the battering rams that aren't there?"

Hector thought for a moment. "Sending them back to Greece where they came from?"

Laughing again, he turned to me.

"I imagine," he said, "they'd be useful for constructing buildings in Greece. Wouldn't you agree your architects would be happy to have them?"

I shook my head. "Many of the Greek construction workers seem to be here, with the army, toiling alongside the shepherds. I doubt the Greeks who stayed home, not even the architects, are building much of anything these days. Agamemnon and the other kings have surely doubled or trebled their taxes by now to pay for this foolish war. Why would the lenders lay out any amount of silver and gold for a construction job with a dubious foreign war going on? I remember the woman who taught me the ways of the world telling me it doesn't matter to lenders how much interest they can charge for a loan if they doubt they'll get their principle back. She said the real interest rate for those loans is zero."

Paris nodded. "They aren't sending those battering rams back to Greece. I've never seen them load any of them on their ships. I've never seen a ship depart the harbor with battering rams on its deck. And that's where they'd have to be."

Hector looked at the harbor again. "Those Greeks are clever. They must be loading the ships at night. And the ships must be departing at night—when you're in bed with your wife thinking about other things."

Paris ignored his brother's innuendo and shook his head. "Why would the Greeks be doing that?"

"Why wouldn't they?" Hector asked. "They don't want us to know they've given up on breaching our walls. They don't want us to know they realize the only way they can win this war is by starving us."

Hector turned to me again.

"But the Greeks don't know," he said, "starving us to death will take them at least ten more years to do—thanks to you and the people working with you in our orchards and gardens. No, the Greek kings will come to their senses and go home well before we starve to death."

Ron Fritsch

Chapter Five

Timon

After our performance in which Lukas sang the song we'd created out of nowhere, Helen asked us to sit with her on the terrace.

"I know you broke all sorts of rules with your song," she said. "I take music lessons with my daughter."

Helen had given birth to one child, Hermione, after she'd returned from Troy and married Menelaus. Helen had persuaded him to sign an order naming Hermione as his heir to the Spartan throne. Helen had almost died giving birth to her and was unable to become pregnant again.

She turned to Lukas and threw her arms around him.

I was pleased to see he didn't resist her embrace.

"I'm glad," she said, releasing him, "you sang about your mother and father. I'd heard you were born in Troy and were only a few months old when they died. I know they didn't go to Troy voluntarily."

Lukas nodded. "They had no wish to participate in that war. But Agamemnon's warriors came and told them and my uncle they'd go to Troy whether they wanted to or not."

"I'm sorry that happened," Helen said. "Menelaus never would've ordered his warriors to do that. Of course, he was never in favor of fighting a war with the Trojans anyway."

That was the first time I'd heard anybody say Menelaus hadn't been in favor of the war. Its purpose, after all, was to rectify a great wrong done to him.

"I'm also very sorry," Helen said, speaking to Lukas, "your mother and father died in Troy. I hope your life in this orphanage hasn't been too grim."

Lukas looked at me and shrugged. "It really hasn't been grim at all. Timon has been my best friend here for as long as I can remember."

Helen turned to me. "You've both chosen well."

"I've never felt," Lukas said, "Timon was a choice. He was always at my side."

I nodded. "Nor did I choose Lukas. As far back as I can remember, we were together."

I could tell our remarks pleased Helen.

"I'm glad," she said, "you're thumbing your noses at the traditional music rules. They never made sense to me. I believe Greece could use some new music, especially personal songs like yours. Do you intend to compose more of them?"

"We do," Lukas replied.

He and I had guessed Helen would come down on our side of the music argument.

Helen

Hector and I paid another visit to Paris in his watchtower. The Greeks had recently pulled their archers back to their encampments, which left the city far beyond their firing range.

"What do you want us to see this time?" Hector asked. "Now that our enemies have admitted their only hope is to starve us to death."

"Look at the harbor," Paris replied. "Do you find anything missing?"

The battering rams were gone.

"I've figured out," Paris said, "what they're doing with their battering rams."

"They're taking them all back to Greece," Hector said. "They no longer care if we know they've given up on breaching our walls or burning us down."

"They aren't taking them back to Greece," Paris said, his voice more emphatic now.

"What do you think they're doing with them?" I asked him.

"They're digging a tunnel," Paris said. "They're using the battering rams to shore it up."

Hector stared at the Greek encampment as if he were seeing it for the first time.

Then he scoffed. "I don't see anything to convince me they're digging a tunnel. Where's the entrance to it? There should be a hole in the ground somewhere, but I don't see one."

"It's in their main tent," Paris replied. "The one they stacked the battering rams next to. They began digging the tunnel inside the tent to conceal from us what they've been doing."

Helen's Orphans

"You're guessing," Hector said. "You don't have any proof they're digging a tunnel."

"What are they doing," I asked Paris, "with the earth they remove from the tunnel?"

"They dump it into the harbor," Paris replied. "The big tent obscures our view of the docks behind it, even from up here. They know that. I'm sure they're dumping the earth from the tunnel there. The waves are gentle, but they're strong enough to move the earth down the sloping floor of the harbor and out into the middle of it where it's deepest. The Greeks know what they're doing. And they damned well know how to hide what they're doing from us."

"Where do you think their tunnel will end?" I asked.

"Just inside the wall here," Paris replied. "They'll know when to stop. I'm sure they've measured the distance between that tent and this entrance more than once. They're Greeks."

"I don't have any doubt," I said, "they'd get that right."

The main entrance to Troy was the part of it closest to the harbor.

Hector shook his head again. "Everything you say is conjecture. You don't have any real proof the Greeks are digging a tunnel. All you've got are some missing battering rams."

"And an excellent understanding," I said, "of the way people determined to get into this city would think. What could get the job done better than a tunnel we can't see?"

"A tunnel that long," Hector said, "would require a lot of digging and earth-moving."

"Those workers the Greeks brought with them," I said, "have nothing else to do now. I'd imagine tunnel-digging and earth-moving would be jobs Agamemnon's warriors could force them to do."

"I thought our archers," Hector said, "killed all of their workers."

Hector's unusual resort to sarcasm startled me.

I turned to Paris. "What would you do to defend the city from Greeks digging a tunnel?"

"I'd divert the stream," Paris said.

The founders of Troy had built it around a stream that rose from a spring inside the eastern wall and ran downhill the length of the city to a sinkhole not far from the main entrance. It was the city's water supply. Hector surely had it as well as the food supply in mind whenever he shrugged off the possibility of a siege lasting ten more years.

35

"You'd divert the stream?" Hector asked Paris. "Where would you have it go?"

"I'd begin digging a ditch today," Paris replied, "between the main entrance and the stream just before it reaches the sinkhole."

Hector scoffed again. "The water would have nowhere to go after it hit the wall here, which would become a dam. You'd create a deep lake all the way back to the sinkhole."

"You're damned right I would," Paris agreed. "And when the Greeks dug their exit for their tunnel under it, the water would flood into it and flush whoever was in it out to the harbor. Then we'd block up the tunnel the same way we did all the other entrances to the city. We'd even use their battering rams to help us do it."

Hector laughed and turned to his brother. "You amuse me. That seems to be your purpose in life. You have a great imagination. You can see the Greeks digging a tunnel all the way from the harbor to our main entrance. You see us flushing them back into the harbor. On a wild guess, you'd divert the stream, create a huge lake and wait for some insidious Greeks to show up."

"I'd hope," I said to Hector, spitting out my words, "you'd consider the tunnel Paris is worried about more than a wild guess. It seems entirely plausible to me. I'd do everything I could to defend against it. I agree with Paris. I'd divert the stream. I'd start doing it today."

Hector shook his head. "I'd never divert the stream. The people would think I'd taken leave of my senses. You're in love with my brother and can't see how impractical he is. I don't blame you for loving him. It's what brought all those Greek armies here and gave us a great opportunity to defeat them. But no fanciful tunnel is going to save them from their folly."

Hector couldn't admit his city might not be as impregnable as he'd believed it was. And without that idea, he couldn't justify his invitation to the Greeks to attack Troy.

He turned to Paris. "Have you spoken of this imaginary tunnel with anybody else?"

Paris shook his head. "I wanted to let you know about it first."

"Good," Hector said. "I don't want either of you mentioning it to a single person. I don't want our people needlessly alarmed by this figment of your imagination."

Helen's Orphans

"I'll do as you wish," Paris said. "But couldn't we at least post some guards at the main entrance here just in case I'm right?"

Hector shook his head again. "The people would wonder why we were doing that, especially now, with the battering rams gone and no more flaming arrows to worry about."

Helen

I remained in the watchtower with Paris after Hector had left us.

"Do you suppose," I asked, "the Greeks pulled their archers back to lull your people into letting down their guard?"

Hector had disbanded the sky-watchers with their blankets and containers of water.

Paris nodded. "You're damned right they did. The Greeks don't want anybody around this entrance when they come out of their tunnel."

I looked at their encampment down by the harbor again. "Their warriors clearly outnumber your warriors. Like two or three to one, I'd say. If you're right about the tunnel, and they break into your city, your people are doomed. Shouldn't you raise the alarm with your fellow Trojans, no matter what Hector wants you to do?"

Paris shook his head. "I've always promised my father and mother I'd never disobey Hector. I made that promise again the day you and I came here from Greece. They'd have no objection to your being here, they told me, as long as you and I were loyal to Hector. He's calm, level-headed, conservative. They like that. I put on performances for the people in athletic competitions. I love applause. I stole the most beautiful woman in the world from a Greek king. My father and mother don't mind my being who I am and doing what I do, but in their eyes I'm not a commander in chief on the same level as Hector."

Timon

"My mother and father," Lukas said, "were helping dig the tunnel at Troy. The tunnel collapsed on them. By the time the other workers uncovered them, they were dead."

Our conversation with Helen on the terrace had gone back to the war in Troy.

"I'm very sorry that happened," Helen said. "I understand a number of people working in the tunnel were killed. Menelaus told me Agamemnon ordered them to keep digging, without waiting until the walls were safely shored up. He was in a hurry to finish the tunnel before the Trojans realized what he was doing."

"Why did he think," I asked, "the Trojans might guess he was digging a tunnel?"

Helen frowned. "The Greeks had taken battering rams to Troy to breach its walls, or at least its entrances. When that failed, Agamemnon was pleased with himself for coming up with the idea to use the battering rams to shore up a tunnel. But he was also aware some clever Trojan might notice the battering rams were missing and guess what the Greeks were doing with them."

"Did some clever Trojan do that," I asked.

Helen frowned again. "Paris did. But his brother Hector paid no attention to him. He didn't want to imagine the Greeks could dig a tunnel all the way from the harbor to, and then under, the walls of Troy. It would destroy his view of the city as invulnerable to any army."

Helen thought for a moment before she continued.

"Agamemnon had once paid a visit to Troy," she said. "The unusual stream there, all of it within the city walls, from the spring where it began to the sinkhole where it disappeared on its way to the harbor, caught his attention. He told Menelaus if he were defending Troy against a tunnel, he'd divert the stream and make the water flow toward the main entrance. That was precisely what Paris wanted to do. But Agamemnon was ready for that. When the workers opened up the tunnel after they were inside Troy, he made certain no warriors were in it."

Lukas shook his head in disgust. "It was okay if workers like my mother and father drowned in the tunnel, but the warriors had to be protected from a clever Trojan who might've figured out what the Greeks were doing?"

Helen nodded. "That was my brother-in-law Agamemnon—as brutal as he was brilliant."

Helen

The horrifying news reached the palace before dawn. At least twenty Greek warriors were already inside the city near the main entrance. Paris and I were still putting on our tunics and sandals when we heard the additional news we didn't need to hear. Like rats in a basement, the Greeks were entering the city from a tunnel they'd dug.

The fighting to determine the fate of Troy had begun by the time Paris and I reached the scene. He chose the roof of a building as a site to fire arrows at Greek warriors and archers far enough behind the front line to ensure a bad shot wouldn't maim or kill a Trojan.

I held a shield for Paris as well as another for myself. Once again, I felt I could justify what I was doing. I wasn't firing an arrow or using a sword or a spear to harm a fellow Greek. I was only protecting a person I loved from injury or death in a senseless war for both sides.

Other Trojan archers and their shield holders joined Paris and me on our roof and on the roofs of nearby buildings. The Trojans fighting with bows and arrows had an advantage over their Greek counterparts. The Trojans could fire down at any Greek warriors or archers careless in the use of their shields. The few archers the Greeks had room for inside Troy could only fire their arrows upward at Trojan archers. Their own warriors were between them and the Trojan warriors fighting on the ground.

During that first day of fighting, the Trojans held the Greek intruders close to the main entrance. The most serious problem for the Greeks was the disposal of their dead and wounded warriors. They had to get them out of the way of their comrades still capable of fighting, but they could only remove them from the battlefield through the tunnel. That traffic slowed to a trickle the replacement warriors coming in the other direction to join the battle.

At sundown Agamemnon had fewer Greek warriors inside the walls of Troy than he'd had at sunrise. During the nighttime lull in the fighting, which brought us our first meal of the day, Paris was among the most vocal in congratulating Hector on successfully holding off the Greeks despite their tunnel—a tunnel Paris had rightly deduced they were digging, a tunnel Hector had stubbornly dismissed as a fantasy.

Loyal Paris clung to his family like a lamb to its mother on the day of its weaning. I wondered if childhood stories of his murdered siblings had anything to do with it.

Ron Fritsch

Chapter Six

Helen

A t dawn the next morning the Trojans learned why the Greeks, despite their losses during the first day of fighting after they'd opened the exit to their tunnel in Troy, nevertheless achieved their paramount goal. They held the main entrance. And during their first night in the city, they quietly unblocked it. They no longer had to depend upon the tunnel alone for the removal of their dead and wounded and the arrival of replacements.

Paris had assumed a tunnel beginning in Agamemnon's tent would end inside the closest entrance to Troy because the Greeks would want to gain control of one as soon as they could.

Still, though, Agamemnon couldn't bring to bear the full weight of his advantage in the war—the far greater number of warriors he had in his army than the Trojans had in theirs. As long as the outnumbered foe could hold its opponents within a limited territory at the main entrance, the one-on-one fighting would result in equal numbers of dead and wounded warriors on both sides. Only after a prolonged period of daily mayhem would the numerical superiority of the Greeks bring them a victory. In the meantime, the Greek warriors, far from home, might grow sick of bloodshed whose only purpose was to sack a beautiful city whose destruction few of them had any personal reason to desire.

"That's our strategy," Hector bravely told the Trojans. "Every day we'll need to kill as many of their warriors as they kill of ours. They have our main entrance now as well as their damned tunnel, but we Trojans have our backs to the wall. We'll fight every day, take our losses and return to the fight the next day because we can do nothing else. Otherwise, we'll cease to exist. We only have ourselves and our city in this world. No sympathetic god or goddess from the tales our ancestors used to tell will save us or the Greeks. They know that as well as we do."

Helen

Achilles and his warriors hadn't yet taken part in the fighting. He and Agamemnon had quarreled over a woman. She'd come to the Greek encampments with other women and men to entertain the warriors. Neither Greek nor Trojan, they did what they did for as much silver, and even in some cases gold, as their customers were willing to pay them.

Achilles had shared his bed with the woman first. But when Agamemnon saw her, he ordered her to share his bed. Whether the woman's desirability or Agamemnon's arrogance was the cause, Achilles decided having her was worth more to him than the outcome of the war.

Despite the unblocked main entrance to the city, the Greeks weren't making any progress against the Trojans. Paris and I could see that from our rooftop position. Many of the Greek warriors thought they'd never win the war without Achilles and his army in it. Some of them even dared to tell Agamemnon they were throwing away their lives for nothing, and they wanted to go home.

When Patroclus, Achilles's companion, learned the Greeks were facing defeat despite their superior numbers, he asked Achilles to let his warriors fight under his command inside Troy. Achilles reluctantly agreed.

Helen

I recognized Patroclus the moment he appeared with his warriors at the entrance to Troy. I'd met him during the festivities in Mycenae after Agamemnon married Clytemnestra. I was there as the sister of the bride and as the bride-to-be of the groom's brother, Menelaus. Patroclus was there as the companion of the king of Phthia, Achilles.

Hector and Patroclus knew what heroes, Greek or Trojan, needed to do. Paris and I watched from the rooftop as they positioned themselves for their duel.

Their combat continued throughout that morning and into the afternoon, along with the one-on-one fighting on either side of them. Then I could see Patroclus begin to stumble. I wondered if his being an invader, with little interest of his own in the outcome of the battle other than pride, was the cause of his fatigue.

Hector, who was defending the lives of his family and kinspeople, found an opportunity during Patroclus's hesitation to end the struggle.

Helen's Orphans

He thrust his spear deep into his adversary's gut and took him down. Then he sliced his sword across Patroclus's throat and finished him off.

A loud cheer went up among the Trojans as the Greeks carried away Patroclus's body.

"Achilles," I told Paris, "might want to make your brother pay for that."

"The fight was fair," Paris said.

"I very much doubt, though, it ended the way Achilles wanted it to."

Helen

Then came the days of Achilles's loud, public grieving for Patroclus. He made a big show of it at the Greek encampment beside the harbor. His warriors continued to fight inside Troy. Without Achilles or Patroclus to lead them, though, they seemed confused. The Greek army had still made no progress against the Trojans.

I didn't doubt Achilles's grief was sincere. On the one occasion I'd spent time with him and Patroclus at my sister's wedding, their love for one another was apparent. But Achilles had made a decision to fight a war. I couldn't imagine he hadn't anticipated Patroclus might be killed in it. Many, many other Greeks had already died outside and inside Troy.

Achilles's initial refusal to fight inside the city because of his spat with Agamemnon, followed by his outlandish display of grief for Patroclus, were sickening reminders the war could've been avoided. If Achilles and his army had remained in Phthia despite my presence in Troy, the other Greek kings and their armies also would've stayed home. The war that brought so much pain and grief to both the Greeks and the Trojans never would've happened.

Timon

The next time Helen came to the orphanage, Lukas and I performed another song we'd composed in the olive grove. I sang and played the lyre. Lukas played the pan flute.

I wakened in a hall of noise
With screaming, laughing, weeping boys.

43

Ron Fritsch

One solemn friend stayed close to me,
And I to him. Security
Is what we sought, but we found more.
I wondered who we were, what for.
War took his kinfolk off to die.
But who were mine, and who was I?

As Lukas had chosen to do with his song, I sang the last two lines of mine twice more for a chorus.

And once again, Helen led the cheering and applause.

Helen

When Achilles, his grieving over, strode through the main entrance to Troy, no Greek or Trojan present needed to be told who he was. The Greek warriors made way for him to go straight to the center of the front line. Hector, on his side, was already there.

Yes, Achilles was an armed intruder in Troy with no good excuse to be there. Yes, Hector was defending the existence of his people and their city with its massive walls, spring-fed stream and verdant orchards and gardens. But Hector had killed the person Achilles had loved the most. Achilles had entered Troy to take revenge.

The combat between Achilles and Hector lasted as long as the duel Menelaus and Paris had faked so well. Achilles and Hector, though, fought as if they knew the outcome of the war depended upon that single day's struggle between them.

I could only imagine it did. If Achilles killed Hector, the Greek warriors would remain in Troy, fight to the end and win the war. If Hector slew Achilles, the Greek warriors would defy Agamemnon, go home with their kings and lose the war.

The more I watched Achilles and Hector thrust and slash at one another, the more I realized how much I preferred the acrobatics of Menelaus and Paris in their thrilling dance together. The duel Achilles and Hector fought, on the other hand, was a raw display of endurance. They both knew one of them would die and lose everything. They both knew the other would live and win the war for his side.

Sunset approached that day when, for whatever reason—I assumed it was nothing more than luck—Hector lost his balance. However brief

44

and slight the slip was, though, Achilles used it to drive his spear into Hector's midsection, just below his ribs. As Hector fell backward from the force of the blow, Achilles rode him to the ground, withdrew his spear and plunged it into his throat, coming close to severing Hector's head from his body.

Helen

As the Greek warriors cheered and proclaimed Achilles the greatest warrior who'd ever fought, Paris and I climbed down from our rooftop and carried Hector's blood-splattered body on a plank to Priam and Hecuba at the entrance to the palace. They stared at Hector's body and repeated, over and over, "Hector's dead." I wondered if their grief had driven them mad.

Helen

Later that night Paris and I went to see Priam and Hecuba in their chamber. Dressed in black like ravens, they'd become coherent enough to speak with us.

Paris asked them to give him command of the Trojan army.

Priam looked as if his son had requested carnal access to his mother.

Hecuba spoke first. "You'd become Achilles's next opponent."

Priam nodded. "Not only that, you'd become his next dead opponent. And we've already lost one son to that thundering Greek."

"We can't possibly lose another," Hecuba agreed. "You must stay on your rooftop, with your bow and arrows and your wife holding your shield. That's how you should seek revenge for Hector's death. Keep your eye on Achilles at all times. We're told your arrows reach their targets far more often than any other Trojan archer's do. Use the skills you have."

"You must play your role," Priam said, "as Troy's most excellent archer."

"Hector's four comrades," Hecuba said, "can command the army."

The four comrades were the warriors Hector ordinarily fought beside. Two, left-handed, were always on his left, and the other two, right-handed, were always on his right. Hector, like Achilles, had fought with both hands.

"I agree," Priam said. "I'll give the four comrades command of the army."

Paris looked at his mother and father as if they'd given him a good spanking, with his tunic lifted and his buttocks bare. "You'll split the command of the Trojan army four ways. An army needs one commander, one voice that can't be questioned in any quarter."

Hecuba shook her head. "Our army's task is basic. Our warriors need to hold the Greeks where they are now. We don't require any more heroic duels."

I'd watched the four comrades in battle. They'd never engage in a heroic duel with Achilles. Hector had trained them to fight defensively and as a team. The five of them would wait patiently until one of their five opponents made a mistake, sometimes so minor most warriors wouldn't notice it. The two comrades closest to that adversary would exact a dear price for the misstep, the error, the miscalculation. They did what they needed to do so quickly their other four adversaries had no chance to take advantage of their momentary numerical superiority against the three comrades who hadn't participated in the takedown. Then it was five comrades against four opponents who had a dead or dying body in their way. That configuration often gave rise to additional worthwhile developments.

"Please let Hector's comrades know," Priam said to Paris, "we've given them command of the Trojan army."

Priam and Hecuba were deeply grieving the loss of their fourth child—this one at the hands of Achilles, no less. But I could find no fault in the decision they made that night.

Timon

When Lukas and I sat with Helen on the terrace after our performance in which I'd sung our new song, she had a question for us. "I know you'll both turn eighteen soon," she said. "Do you have plans for what you'll do when you leave the orphanage?"

"We'll look for work in an olive grove," Lukas replied. "We've heard jobs are available."

"They'll need to hire us both," I said. "We want to stay together for the rest of our lives."

Helen nodded. "I hope you do."

Helen's Orphans

"We'll save our earnings," Lukas said, "and buy our own olive grove as soon as we can. We'll look for a small one we can add to later."

I nodded. "We intend to offer the most delicious olives and oil in Greece."

"We'll do whatever we need to do," Lukas said, "to sell everything we produce."

Lukas was down to earth and practical. According to him, I was a dreamer.

"I have a proposal for you," Helen said. "The couple currently in charge of the royal olive grove are elderly. They were managing the grove before the war. They believe it's time for them to retire. We understand they have substantial savings, and they'll receive a pension from us. They shouldn't have any financial worries."

Helen paused. I was eager to hear what she intended to say next. I could already tell, though, Lukas saw trouble ahead.

"I've told Menelaus," Helen said, "how well the two of you have managed the olive grove here. We'd like to put you in charge of the royal olive grove. We'd pay you what we're paying the couple managing it now. We also have a chamber in the palace you can live in."

When that day began, I hadn't imagined Lukas and I would be the recipients of such good news. Helen was offering to take us from the orphanage to a chamber in the palace. We'd be working on behalf of the people of Sparta. Menelaus and Helen spent the proceeds from everything they produced on the palace grounds to support the orphans and the people unable to work. Most of the individuals in both groups had been victims of the war.

But the deep frown on Lukas's face told me he didn't consider Helen's proposal the opportunity I took it to be. He'd be living in a palace and having day-to-day contact with a person he felt was responsible for the untimely deaths of his mother and father.

He looked at me as if he envied me for not having a story of parents whose deaths at an early age in an ugly, foolish war could never be forgiven.

He turned to Helen. "Can we think about your offer?"

"It's so sudden," I said, exposing how giddy I was, "so unexpected."

"Of course," Helen said, "you should give our offer some very serious thought. Menelaus and I had assumed you'd want to do that."

Ron Fritsch

Chapter Seven

Helen

F or more than a month the Trojans were able to hold the front line where it had been when Achilles killed Hector. Then, it seemed to me, a perception took hold among the Trojans that the Greeks would never give up on their war without a total victory, and the day would come when the greater number of Agamemnon's fighters would make all the difference in the world. In the meantime, the daily slaughter on both sides would continue.

The Greek warriors began moving the front line further into Troy. And as the line moved away from the narrow confines near the main entrance to the city, it lengthened and required more warriors on both sides to maintain positions on it.

Paris and I, along with the other Trojan archers and their shield holders, had to leave our initial firing positions inside Troy and move to the roofs of buildings further from the main entrance. As soon as we did that, though, the Greek archers took over the rooftops we gave up, and the defenders of Troy lost a valuable advantage. Greek archers could now include among their targets any Trojan ground warriors who ventured within their range. Those who were careless with their shields, even for a moment or two, could take an arrow.

I detected a growing sense of doom among the Trojan warriors. And soon after that, I felt it wherever I went among the people of Troy.

Helen

The Trojan front line began retreating almost every day, sometimes the length of an adult human body, sometimes the length of five or six laid end to end. The Trojans who weren't fighting—the adults who could no longer fight and the children who couldn't fight yet—spent parts of their days digging graves in the orchards and groves and, following the after-sunset funerals, parts of their nights helping the warriors cover their comrades with the earth piled next to the graves.

I could imagine the Trojans giving in to panic, throwing down their arms and surrendering to the Greeks. But the people I was living with refused to do that.

"Those Greeks, that Agamemnon," Hecuba said, "would kill us all."

"We have to fight them to the end," Priam said, "to the last day Troy exists."

Paris and I had brought to their chamber the only food we or they ate that day.

"I heard some people talking about making an escape," I said.

I'd helped those people prepare the food many Trojans would consume that night, after the funerals.

"Escape?" Hecuba asked.

"Escape would be treachery," Priam said.

Paris turned to me. "What did you hear them say?"

"When we're down to the end," I said, "they believe the survivors should unblock the eastern entrance near the spring. They say there aren't many Greeks in that direction. You can see that, they say, from the watchtower."

"After they unblock the entrance," Paris asked, "then what will they do?"

"They'll ride out of here in every chariot and carriage they can lay their hands on. They'll draw straws to see who'll ride in a chariot and who'll ride in a carriage."

The horses could pull the chariots faster than the carriages. The riders in the carriages, though, would have more protection from any Greek archers who chased them.

"Assuming they successfully escape," Paris asked, "where will they go?"

"They'll go south, along the coast, to the ships."

Before the Greeks had arrived, Hector had ordered a group of older warriors to sail the Trojan fleet to a harbor far to the south and keep it there. The Trojans talking about escape assumed the Greek navy hadn't searched for the fleet. The Greek sailors appeared to have been too busy throughout the war resupplying Agamemnon's army of warriors and workers to have time for anything else. Hector hadn't intended to provide the Trojans with a means of escape—he'd never considered they'd need one—but he might've done it anyway.

"What will they do with the ships?" Paris asked.

Helen's Orphans

This was, to me, the most intriguing part of the escape plan. "They'll go west, south of Greece, to Italy. They think they can build a new Troy there."

I confess I'd enjoyed speaking with the people who couldn't stop talking of an escape. Whether it was to Italy or some other place, an escape was the only real hope I could imagine the Trojans had left.

Hecuba and Priam, though, stared at me as if I were a child who'd spoken nonsense.

"I'll never leave Troy," Hecuba said.

"I'll die here," Priam said. "There will never be another Troy."

"If, at the end, though," Paris asked his mother and father, "those people still wished to attempt to make an escape, would you order them not to?"

Hecuba and Priam looked at one another and simultaneously shook their heads.

"No," Hecuba replied. "I'd let them go wherever they wanted to go."

"So would I," Priam said. "But I'd never go with them."

Helen

I had a question for Paris as soon as we returned to our chamber and could speak privately. "What will you and I do at the end, after we've lost all hope for saving Troy?"

Paris thought for a moment. "I can't leave my mother and father here by themselves."

"So you'll stay in Troy with them? You'll let Agamemnon torture the three of you before he has you killed—for the amusement of his victorious, drunken warriors?"

Paris shook his head. "No. If I have to, I'll force my mother and father to go with us. I'll ask my guards to put them in a carriage and keep them in it until after we've made our getaway. I'm sure my guards will do that. They won't want their king and queen left to the mercy of Agamemnon. My mother and father will thank me later. They'll agree I did the right thing."

Timon

"We need to see my uncle Nestor," Lukas said.

We were walking to the dining hall for supper with the other orphans who'd worked with us in the olive grove that day.

"We should see him again," I said.

"He lost his brother, sister-in-law and left foot in a stupid war Helen brought down on Sparta, on all of Greece. How do you suppose he'd take it if he heard his nephew had become one of her favorites and accepted her invitation to spend his days in her palace?"

"Do you think he's still living on your family's property?"

"Where else would he be?"

"Do you suppose he's still unmarried?"

"He would've let me know if he got married. He would've invited me to the wedding."

He'd told Lukas and me no woman in her right mind would want a shepherd missing a foot. She'd be too afraid, he said, she'd end up doing all the work they'd need to do.

When Lukas's parents died in Troy, Nestor inherited the family pastures. If he died without a spouse or children, the land would pass to Lukas.

We'd reached the middle of the summer. Our work in the olive grove was caught up. We were more than old enough to leave the orphanage on our own for a while. Lukas's ancestral hills were a three-day walk from the orphanage. The kitchen workers would give us food we could take with us in our backpacks. We'd find ripe berries growing wild along the road. The orphanage berry patches were producing abundant amounts of fruit that year.

"I agree with you," I said. "We should go see your uncle."

Helen

Hector's four comrades commanding the Trojan army hadn't yet given up on saving Troy. Paris and I therefore continued spending our days on one rooftop or another. He was still attempting to kill every Greek he could.

I felt I had to remain at his side. I was certain nobody else could hold his shield for him as well as I did. Nobody else had nearly as much practice doing it as I had.

By then, though, the many killings and injuries on both sides had become a nightmare waking in the morning and facing another day of them only made more frightful. I had no doubt the Trojans had lost the war. The Greeks still suffered as many deaths and injuries each day as the Trojans did, but I couldn't see them giving up and going home without the victory they'd sailed to Troy for.

They believed those who survived and returned to Greece as victors would be considered heroes for the remainder of their lives. And all those still fighting could only imagine, until the moment they fell, they'd survive and return to Greece. It would do them no good to suppose they could become another instance of what they saw daily— fallen comrades tasting their own blood, knowing at last they'd given everything they had for nothing.

Paris kept himself positioned on rooftops near the center of the front lines. He didn't need to tell me why he did that. He wanted to take down Achilles.

"What will the death of Achilles accomplish now?" I asked, holding our shields.

"Achilles killed my brother," Paris replied.

"So his death will accomplish revenge."

"Call it whatever you will."

"He fought a fair fight with your brother."

"I agree. It was a fair fight."

"Then why not let it be? You met Achilles. He might have an inflated opinion of himself, but he's far from being the worst person in the world. He's no Agamemnon. He's not the uncle who murdered your sister and brothers before you were born."

Paris had his arrow aimed at Achilles as we spoke. "He killed my brother, the only brother I knew. I don't feel I have a choice. I'd dishonor my mother and father if I didn't attempt to kill the Greek invader who killed Hector."

I shook my head. "I've seen far too many people, Trojans and Greeks, killed and injured in this war."

Paris took his eyes off Achilles and looked at me. "What would you do if you were me?"

The answer to that question was on my lips as soon as I heard it.

"Tonight," I replied, "I'd ask the surviving Trojans to pack up all their chariots and carriages with whatever they have of value they can take with them. Tomorrow night I'd ask them to hitch their horses to their chariots and carriages, unblock the eastern entrance to the city and ready themselves to make a run for it at dawn the next day."

"What if my brother's four comrades told the people not to do what I'd asked them to do? What if the four comrades said the war must go on?"

"I'd remind them you're the surviving prince in this kingdom, the king and the queen are too crippled with grief to rule and, if you had to, you'd order the people to do what you requested them to do."

"Do you believe the people would obey me?"

"I have no doubt about it. They would."

Paris shook his head. "There's a flaw in your argument."

"What's that?"

"My mother and father aren't too grief-stricken to rule Troy. And I'd rather die than stoop to treason."

Paris turned to Achilles again, looking for any opportunity to take a shot.

Timon

Lukas and I selected villages along the way to his family's sunlit hills to stay overnight in. We went to each house and informed the townspeople we'd be singing for our supper in the village center. After we finished our performances, we had to choose among the offers of food and lodging we received.

The two men we stayed with the second night—they had the grandest house in the village by far—apparently assumed our entertainment for them would consist of more than singing in the village center. But we were glad we only had to say no once and didn't have to deal with a retaliatory request from them to leave.

In fact, before we departed the next morning, our hosts asked us to stay with them again on our way back to the orphanage. When Lukas and I talked about their request later that day, we both wondered if they were hoping we might change our minds about joining them in their bed. We decided we'd better select another village to sing in on our return.

Helen

Helen's Orphans

The war, which seemed to me even more absurd now than it was when it began, continued. The Greeks buried their dead in the sea. The Trojans buried theirs under the trees in the orchards and groves I loved. I hoped my fellow Greeks, after they won the war, would refrain from destroying those happy places, and whoever later occupied the city once called Troy would be able to use and enjoy them as the people I'd lived with had.

The Greek archers were well aware Paris was concentrating his attention on Achilles.

"You've got to try harder," I said to him, "to remain behind my shield."

The Greeks had pushed us back to yet another rooftop position. Paris had developed a bad habit in his determination to hit his target. Before he fired an arrow, he'd briefly step away from the shield I held for him and leave himself exposed. I could only assume at least some of the Greek archers had seen him do it.

"What difference does it make now?" he asked.

"It could mean the difference between your life and your death."

"What difference would my death make? The Greeks have won this war. Nobody knows that better than you. Nobody can save Troy now. You've told me that yourself."

"Your death would make a great difference to me. I love you. I don't want to see you die. I want to escape with you from Agamemnon and his armies. I want to get on a ship with you and go to Italy. I want to help you and your people rebuild this beautiful city somewhere else. I'd love to plant and tend their orchards, vineyards, groves and gardens. I'd wish to go beyond what my fellow Greeks have done with theirs. I'd hope to put them to shame. And if you were there with me, I could do it. You'd help me do it."

Ron Fritsch

Chapter Eight

Timon

Pointing his finger at the sunlit but mostly rocky slopes of the surrounding hills, Uncle Nestor showed us the extent of the pastures he'd inherited when his brother and sister-in-law died in Troy. The sheep and goats that roamed the land, though, weren't his.

"Neighbors," Nestor said, "pay me a pittance to let their sheep and goats eat their fill on my land."

When he'd returned from Troy, he explained, he discovered the person his brother and sister-in-law had hired to tend their sheep and goats while they were gone had absconded with them instead. Nestor had hoped to start new herds, but that day hadn't yet arrived.

"Not with one foot still in Troy," he told us.

His only other income was the pension he received each month from the Spartan treasury for his injury in the war. It hadn't taken Lukas and me long after our arrival to understand why Nestor had never offered to remove his nephew from the orphanage and care for him in their family's now dilapidated home.

Nestor appeared not to have cut his hair or trimmed his beard for a number of months. When he removed his threadbare clothes to bathe in a sunny brook with Lukas and me, we could see he had precious little fat or muscle between his skin and bones. He looked much older than we knew he was.

Helen

Paris had his arrow aimed at Achilles.

"When he thrusts his spear overhanded," Paris said, "he lowers his shield and leaves the upper left corner of his breast unprotected. It's like that only for a moment, but if I time my shot just right, I can hit him. For my dead brother's sake, I've at least got to try."

"Whatever you do," I said, "it won't bring your brother back to life. You wanted to divert the stream. That could've saved him from the wrath of Achilles. But Hector was stubborn. He wanted to go on believing Troy was perfectly safe behind its massive walls, and the

Greeks wouldn't dare dig a tunnel under them. He wouldn't listen to a naysayer like you."

Nor would Hector's brother Paris listen to a naysayer like me.

Timon

Lukas stoned a duck on a pond in the hills. I removed my clothes again and swam out to retrieve the unlucky fowl. Nestor plucked its feathers. He'd use them for a new pillow, he told us. Then he cut the bird open, emptied its innards, saving only its heart and liver, and began roasting it over his fire for our supper. Lukas took a knife to some of our onions and loaves of bread and tossed the pieces in the bowl Nestor had positioned to catch drippings from the bird. The fat seemed to be just what our host needed to remain alive.

As we waited for the duck to cook, Lukas turned to his uncle and got to the point.

"You told us at the orphanage," he said, "you knew for a fact Helen freely ran off with Paris and started the war."

Nestor grimaced. "I saw her do it."

"You saw her?" Lukas asked, wide-eyed. "You saw her doing what?"

Nestor stared at the fire. "I saw her running off with Paris."

"You saw her yourself?" Lukas asked.

Nestor nodded. "I saw her myself."

"How did that come about?" Lukas persisted.

Nestor sighed as if he'd witnessed a vicious murder he had no wish to recall.

"She was supposed to marry King Menelaus that day," Nestor said. "He'd followed the custom and laid out food and wine on the palace grounds the previous day for anybody who wanted it. He had musicians for singing and dancing. All the young people in Sparta showed up at the palace. I was no exception. Your father and mother had encouraged me. They told me I didn't want to miss a king's wedding festivities. The next time a king got married, they said, I'd be too old to attend. They were wrong. The next time a king got married in Sparta, I wasn't too old, but I was missing a foot. Menelaus didn't put out any food or wine for that one anyway."

The next time a king got married in Sparta was when Helen came home from Troy and kept her promise, at long last, to wed Menelaus.

58

Helen's Orphans

"I saw her in the twilight just before dawn on the wedding day," Nestor said. "I admit I'd stayed up all night drinking the king's wine. I was with two other shepherd boys from these hills who didn't have any more sense than I had. We'd never been that close to the palace before, and we knew we'd never be there again."

Nestor turned to Lukas and laughed.

"I was an orphan like you," he said. "The only father I had then was my brother, who became your father, and he was only a year older than me."

"What did you see," Lukas asked, "at dawn that day?"

"I saw Helen and Paris," Nestor replied.

"You saw them?" Lukas asked. "Where did you see them, and what were they doing?"

Uncle Nestor shuddered. "They were running across the palace lawn together. They were leaving the palace. He wasn't forcing her to do anything. He didn't have a weapon on him. Neither did she. His guards weren't with them. They were alone."

Lukas turned to me with narrowed eyes and shook his head.

"How did you know," I asked Nestor, "the people running across the lawn were Helen and Paris?"

"I'd seen them the day before," Nestor replied. "Helen was on a balcony with the king waving to the crowd. Paris was in the crowd with some other Trojans—his guards I was told. Everybody knew who he was. He was the Trojan prince. His father and mother, the king and queen of Troy, and his older brother Hector had sent him to the wedding. He was supposed to be an honored guest. Instead, he ran off with the bride. Can you imagine the nerve it took him to do that? And not just him. Her too. I mean, both of them should've won some sort of prize for audacity the morning I saw them. Helen was supposed to marry the king that day. And Paris was an enemy prince Menelaus had invited to his wedding. And off the bride and the guest ran together. I couldn't believe what I saw."

"How did you know," I asked, "they were leaving the palace?"

"After they entered the woods at the end of the lawn," Nestor replied, "I got up on my feet somehow, drunken as I was, and followed them. At a distance, so they wouldn't see me. They met the other Trojans, the guards, in the woods. They got in their carriage with them. They rode off toward the harbor where people said the Trojan ship was anchored.

Helen didn't put up any resistance at all. She was on her way to Troy. And neither she nor her pretty boyfriend Paris gave a damn what happened to anybody else."

"Were the two other shepherds with you then?" I asked.

Nestor shook his head. "They were too damned drunk by that time of the day to get up off their asses. I wasn't as drunk as they were."

"What happened to those shepherd boys?" I asked. "Are they still alive?"

Nestor shook his head again. "They died a long time ago. One died in Troy."

"One of the shepherds died in Troy?" Lukas asked. "What happened to the other one?"

Nestor was focused on the fire again. "Odysseus did him in. After the sack of Troy, that hero needed as many shepherd boys as he could lay his hands on to sail his ships back to Ithaca. His warriors got us drunk on wine. We were already out to sea when we woke up. They threw me off the ship I was on as soon as they saw I was missing a foot. I wasn't so far out, though, I couldn't swim back to shore, hungover as I was. My friend wasn't so lucky. They kept him on the damned ship. He died on it, too."

"How did he die?" I asked.

Nestor winced again. "People said the war had driven Odysseus mad. He was worried he'd been away from Ithaca so long his wife Penelope had surely taken a lover. He dreaded arriving home only to discover she'd shared his bed with another person. He'd have to kill her and her lover and everybody else who knew anything about it."

"How did that get your friend killed," Lukas asked.

"Odysseus began hallucinating," Nestor replied. "He saw one-eyed monsters nobody else could see. He heard mermaids calling to him. You can imagine what he said they wanted. And he dismissed out of hand what everybody else could see. As a result, he defied every storm he came across. He made no attempt to ride them out in the nearest port. He sailed into them headfirst. One of them sank the ship my friend was on. Nobody saw him again."

"How do you know," Lukas asked, "what happened to him?"

Nestor couldn't take his eyes off the flames. "One of the shepherd boys from these hills survived his time with Odysseus. After the bloodshed in Ithaca, they didn't need him anymore and sent him home.

Helen's Orphans

He gets by herding sheep and goats for other people. He'll tell you the story of sailing from Troy to Ithaca with Odysseus. He talks of little else. Women don't want him for a husband any more than they want me. I suppose we should be glad we've got each other."

"Why didn't Menelaus come to the rescue of his shepherd boys?" I asked. "Why did he let Odysseus abduct them?"

Nestor shook his head. "It wasn't the fault of Menelaus. He hadn't forced us to go to Troy. Agamemnon did that. And when the war was over, he let Odysseus abduct as many Spartan shepherds as he wanted. Agamemnon must've owed him a debt for something."

"There was no way," I asked, "you could complain to your own king?"

Nestor laughed. "Menelaus was inside the walls of Troy after the fighting had stopped and the surviving Trojans had fled. He was looking for Helen. She was why we'd fought the war. He had to bring her home. I thought as soon as she was back in Sparta, he'd have her executed for being the traitor she was. Instead, he forgave her, married her and made her the queen. I can't imagine anybody has ever loved another person more than he loved her. You know, he didn't send the warriors to take the shepherds to Troy. Those were his brother's warriors. Back in those days, Agamemnon bossed everybody around, even Achilles and Odysseus. All the Greek kings did what he told them to do. And look what it got us."

Nestor stared at the end of his leg where his missing foot would've been if Agamemnon's warriors hadn't put him on a ship bound for Troy.

Nestor's story had left me with a question. "After you and your two friends saw Helen and Paris running across the palace lawn, did you tell anybody else what you saw?"

"Hell, no," Nestor replied. "We didn't dare tell anybody else."

"Why not?"

Nestor looked at me as if I'd asked him whether the sun rose in the west.

"Agamemnon," he said, "would've ordered his warriors to kill us. By the time we slept ourselves sober that afternoon, we heard Agamemnon had told the other kings the Trojan prince had viciously abducted Helen. If we'd told anybody we'd seen her running off with that prince of her own free will, we would've been calling Agamemnon a liar. He had a lot of his warriors at the palace that day. No, we didn't dare tell anybody what we saw that morning."

"After the war was over and Agamemnon was murdered," I asked, "did you tell anybody then what you saw?"

Nestor shook his head. "By that time Helen was the queen of Sparta. I was living off the pension she and Menelaus gave me for my missing foot. You can't see the blood on those few pieces of silver their people bring me every month, but it's there anyway. Helen knows she was responsible for all the deaths and injuries in that damned war. But I wasn't about to jeopardize my pension by casting aspersions on her. Until now, I haven't told anybody what I saw the morning Helen and Paris ran off to Troy. I hope I can trust both of you not to repeat to anybody else what you've heard me say. I just don't want any trouble at this time in my life."

"You can trust us," I said, "not to repeat your story."

"Yeah," Lukas said, "we'll keep our mouths shut."

Helen

One bright morning at the end of my last summer in Troy, when I should've been in an orchard, vineyard, grove or garden helping with the harvest, Paris fired his arrow and hit his target. But, having stepped away from my shield entirely in order to get off his best possible shot, he took a Greek arrow deep in his gut.

The arrow Paris had fired must have forced itself between two of Achilles's ribs and pierced his heart. Within a moment his wound was spurting blood, and he fell to the ground.

The Trojan warriors near him could see, as I could, he was doomed. They sent up a cheer.

After one of Paris's guards on our rooftop shouted down to them the identity of the archer who'd shot Achilles, the cheers from all the Trojans became his name. "Paris! Paris! Paris!"

But that hero lay flat on his back with blood of his own flowing from his wound like wine from an upended decanter.

He looked up at me and managed a twisted grin. "Don't cry," he said. "Please don't cry."

I wondered if he imagined this last victory would be his greatest, the one everybody in the years to come who heard the story of the Trojan

Helen's Orphans

War would never forget. Neither he nor I could know then his running off to Troy with me would win him that honor.

I leaned down and kissed him on his lips. He was, as his detractors would never let you forget, a physically beautiful man. But he wasn't the fool they used that circumstance to imply he also was. Although he never took any credit for it, he'd figured out, alone among the Trojans, the Greeks were using their battering rams to dig a tunnel. What he saw could've saved Troy.

But now he lay ruined, his lovely body mutilated forever by an enemy arrow he could've avoided. I kissed him again on his lips and realized he'd stopped breathing. I couldn't detect a pulse. I closed his eyes.

He and I had both understood we were moving in opposite directions. He'd brought down Achilles, at a great risk to his own life, to maintain what he thought was the honor of his family. I'd hoped he, unlike his brother and Achilles and the other heroes, wouldn't find it necessary to do that. But I could no more recast the loyal son and brother and pursuer of gossamer glory he was than I could turn the reflection of the sun on the sea into gold.

I, though, wished to hold my shield steady at all times and live on in a world in which heartbreak was the order of the day but moments of happiness were possible nevertheless.

Ron Fritsch

Chapter Nine

Timon

Lukas and I were on our way back to the orphanage the day after we and his uncle had feasted on roast duck.

He asked me the question I knew he'd ask. "Do you think my uncle was telling us the truth?"

"I'm certain your uncle is an honest person."

"That doesn't answer my question. Nestor admitted he'd been drinking all that night and the previous day. He was the same age you and I are now. He could've imagined he saw Helen and Paris running off together in the dim light at dawn—after he woke up that afternoon and learned they'd sailed to Troy. The other two shepherd boys he was with are no longer alive to confirm whether his story is true or not."

We stopped to replenish our supply of berries.

I had a question of my own for Lukas. "Do you believe your uncle was telling us the truth?"

"I think he was. He supplied some details that made his story sound as if it was true. Helen and Paris ran across the lawn and through the woods. They were in a hell of a hurry to get away before they got caught. They rode off in the carriage with the guards who came to Sparta with Paris. They went in the direction of the harbor where the Trojan ship was."

"I think you're right. Those details do make your uncle's story ring true. But what about Menelaus? Despite what Helen did that morning, he married her after the war and made her the queen of Sparta."

Lukas snickered. "The poor guy was still in love with her. And he still is now, many years later. You can see it when he comes to the orphanage with her."

"I agree with you about that too. It's obvious he adores her."

Lukas threw an overripe berry at me, striking me as he'd intended, in the upper-left quadrant of my bare chest. That was where people said Paris's arrow had pierced Achilles's heart.

"And when the war was over and Paris was dead," Lukas continued his argument, "she had only one option left if she wanted to remain alive. That was to marry Menelaus."

I finished wiping the splattered berry off my chest with some leaves.

"Helen always seems to me," I said, "as much in love with Menelaus as he is with her."

Lukas scoffed. "She's a great actor. She could play anybody who was supposed to be in love with somebody else. She could play you or me."

I glared at him. "That's unfair. I don't think she's acting. I think she loves the guy."

Lukas shrugged. "You would think that. You've always been partial to Helen. She can do no wrong in your eyes."

"Being fair to her doesn't mean I believe she never did anything wrong."

"But if what my uncle told us is the truth, how can you expect me to live in the palace with her?"

We finished picking berries and resumed walking down the road.

"If we don't go live in the palace with Helen," I said, "we'll be giving up a wonderful opportunity. Not too many orphans get a chance to manage the royal olive grove."

We walked in silence past a field of ripening wheat rising and falling in the breeze like waves in a golden sea.

"We've got to be brave," I said. "We've got to ask Helen for her side of the story."

Lukas shook his head. "I doubt she wants to talk about that part of her life anymore. Especially with a couple of orphan boys."

"Well, then, if she won't explain how she ended up in Troy, we'll have to let her know why we can't accept her offer. We'll tell her we've got to assume she's responsible for what happened to your mother, father and uncle, and accepting her offer wouldn't be right."

Lukas turned to me. "That's what we'll have to do."

Helen

Paris's guards and I carried his body to Priam and Hecuba at the entrance to the palace. They clung to one another.

"Do with us as you will," Hecuba said to Hector's comrades, Paris's guards and me.

"Our five children are all dead now," Priam said. "Agamemnon's army will destroy our city. We've nothing left to live for. No king and queen have sunk as low as we have."

Helen's Orphans

Helen

That night, with the comrades and guards in charge, the surviving Trojans loaded their chariots and carriages. The next night they unblocked the eastern entrance and left the city. They took Priam, Hecuba and all the silver and gold in the royal treasury with them.

The comrades and guards told me they were going south along the coast to find the Trojan fleet. I agreed to tell the Greeks the surviving Trojans told me they were going north along the coast to find their fleet.

Helen

I walked to my favorite orchard with the few possessions I'd need for my journey home to Sparta. I sat down on a grassy knoll and waited.

Greek warriors found me there. They knew who I was as soon as they saw me. They sent a messenger to Menelaus, who wasted no time coming to get me.

When our ship bound for Sparta left the harbor, we could see Troy was in flames.

"Agamemnon did that," Menelaus told me. "He insisted the city had to be destroyed."

Helen

Menelaus married me on the day of our return. After the loss in the war of so many Spartans and other Greeks, to say nothing of the Trojans, it was no time, he and I agreed, for any kind of wedding festivities.

Helen

Unlike Odysseus, Agamemnon hadn't given any indication he worried his wife and queen Clytemnestra had taken a lover in his absence. And unlike Penelope, Clytemnestra had shared her marital bed with a lover, one she claimed was more beautiful than both Menelaus and Paris. I neither saw him nor asked anybody who had seen him if Clytemnestra was right. She'd spared him from duty in Troy with the other most able Greek workers. She'd heard the stories the people told about the dispute between Agamemnon and Achilles over a woman.

Upon Agamemnon's return to Mycenae, Clytemnestra informed him her lover was a servant she'd hired. That much of her story was true.

The lover prepared a bath for Agamemnon. After the king, who'd destroyed Troy at an expense in human lives and silver and gold even the Greeks couldn't measure, lay down in his bath, the lover threw a net over him as if he were a hapless fish caught in the sea.

So entangled, Agamemnon could make no defense as the lover approached him with a butcher knife.

But the great king could scream for help to his guards outside the door to his chamber. They couldn't respond to his cries, though, before his unfaithful wife's lover had driven his knife between the king's ribs and into his heart.

When the guards reached the scene, the queen's bloodied lover gripped the knife with both of his hands above the bath for what appeared to them to be a second stabbing attempt.

Having caught the lover-servant in the act of committing a regicide, the guards took turns hacking at his neck with their swords until his head fell loose from his body and dropped into the crimson bath between his naked victim's thighs.

Timon

When Lukas and I returned to the orphanage after our visit to his uncle, we discovered a messenger from Helen had arrived in our absence.

The message was an invitation to visit her at the palace. She said we could arrive any day we chose. Before the messenger left, we gave her the date we planned to show up.

Our music instructors were certain Helen wanted us to sing privately for Menelaus and Hermione. And if we did, and if the king and princess enjoyed hearing us as much as Helen had, would we put in a good word for the people who'd trained us so well?

"Of course we will," I said.

I knew Lukas could never bring himself to promise he'd say anything so preposterous. I also knew I'd do it no matter how darkly he'd scowl at me as I did it.

We began our walk to the palace the next morning. We arrived early in the afternoon two days later.

Helen's Orphans

Helen

Clytemnestra insisted she'd played no part in the murder of her unfaithful husband by her lover. Menelaus and I assumed, as other Greeks did, she'd asked her lover to kill Agamemnon but hadn't anticipated he'd commit the murder in such a clumsy manner. Using silver and gold from the Mycenean treasury, to which Clytemnestra had unlimited access, to hire an expert and discreet poisoner would've made far more sense than a netting and stabbing in a bath within earshot of armed guards.

In any event, nobody in Mycenae came forward to defend their queen. She'd ruled the kingdom during the years Agamemnon was in Troy. Even without the excessive taxes to support the war and the frequent news of loved ones injured and killed across the sea, that wouldn't have been a happy time for most Myceneans. Early on, Clytemnestra let the people know how she'd decide who the winners and losers would be in almost every dispute that came before her. The parties who offered her, through her underlings, more in silver and gold would win. The parties who offered her less, or nothing, would lose.

Myceneans envied their neighbors in Sparta. Before Menelaus had departed for Troy, he'd appointed three citizens, two women and one man, who were admired for their wisdom and rectitude, to rule as regents in his absence. In case they were nevertheless tempted to do what Clytemnestra chose to do, Menelaus let them know he considered bribe-taking a form of treason.

After Agamemnon's assassination, his and Clytemnestra's two-year-old son Orestes became the king. In normal times the closest relative of a child, in this case his mother, would've ruled as a regent, or would've appointed others to act as regents. Agamemnon had chosen the latter course during the regency for Menelaus, although those regents made no ruling without first gaining Agamemnon's approval.

Clytemnestra had no opportunity to rule for Orestes. The highest commanders of the Mycenean army placed her under arrest, although they left her in the palace with enough servants to keep it in good order and her alive. The commanders also asked Menelaus, as the sole uncle of Orestes, to act as the regent. Menelaus agreed to do so but only if I also became a regent who had equal say with him in the matters of

Mycenae. He reminded the commanders I was Orestes's aunt and as closely related to the boy as he was. The commanders agreed.

Menelaus and I often traveled to Mycenae to carry out our duties as regents for Orestes. We heard the people's complaints in a house owned by one of the high army commanders and his companion, the heir to a shipping fortune. The house was as commodious as the palace.

After servants at the palace informed us Clytemnestra was neglecting Orestes, we ordered him removed from her custody. We took him back to Sparta to live with us as if he were our son.

During our visits to Mycenae, Menelaus and I would often inspect the palace to make certain the servants were providing Clytemnestra with everything she needed to live comfortably. During our first visits, we attempted to speak with her, but she told us we had nothing to say to her, and she had nothing to say to us.

"You've won," she'd say, looking at me and shrugging as if it were a dreary matter of fact, "and I've lost."

Within a few days, the assassination of Agamemnon, the arrest of Clytemnestra and the commencement of the regency for Orestes had turned the world upside down for Menelaus and me. We went from being a king and queen with no army and no treasury to a royal couple with two of each. We intended to use them for the benefit of the people of the two kingdoms the unpredictable accidents of history had placed in our charge. We hoped in later years historians would look back on the events of that time and say the people had won, and royal brutality and corruption had lost.

Helen

Menelaus and I chose not to determine Clytemnestra's ultimate fate. She was, after all, the boy-king Orestes's mother.

As soon as he was old enough to understand such matters, we told him what had happened. We made it clear to him he'd decide what to do with her when he turned eighteen. He could place her on trial, or he could pardon her and let her go free. Until then, she'd remain under guard in the palace in Mycenae. We also told Clytemnestra that's how we'd proceed with her.

After we removed Orestes from her custody and brought him to Sparta to live with us, she refused to see him again. We never

70

Helen's Orphans

understood why. We thought she'd attempt to befriend her son in order to win a finding of not guilty or a pardon from him when he became of age, but she chose not to do that.

The first thing Orestes did when he turned eighteen and became the ruling king of Mycenae was, from that time forward, the subject of endless conversations among all the Greeks. He placed his mother on trial for taking bribes and assassinating Agamemnon, found her guilty on all charges and ordered her execution. She chose to drink hemlock.

The Myceneans celebrated the day my sister Clytemnestra died as if it were a holiday. She represented the bad old days to them—the Trojan War years.

I found no reason to celebrate, no matter what she'd done. She and I had grown up in a repugnant setting, but she refused to let it defeat her. She left an orphanage to marry a king and become a queen. Her main achievement—for Menelaus, me and every other Greek—was the assassination of Agamemnon. I would've pardoned her for that crime.

She'd also taught me, far more than I'd wanted to admit in my youth, how to survive. From her point of view, which was the only one that mattered to her, she was right. She'd lost, and I'd won.

I only wished, though, she'd learned to be kinder.

Ron Fritsch

Chapter Ten

Timon

When Lukas and I reached the palace, Helen walked with us to the royal olive grove, which was at least triple the size of the orphanage grove.

"It's beautiful," Lukas said.

I turned to Helen. "Would we do our work under your supervision?"

She laughed. "I'd work under your supervision. The people Menelaus and I appoint to manage the royal gardens, orchards, vineyards and groves supervise us whenever we work in their domains. That's usually when they're busy and need all the workers they can get."

I hadn't imagined a king and a queen would wish to do such work. The look on Lukas's face told me he hadn't either.

We sat on wooden chairs Helen had arranged in a triangle in the shade of one of the larger olive trees in the grove. We could refill our cups with cold water at a nearby well.

"Lukas and I want to ask you some questions," I said. "We need the answers before we can accept or reject your offer to us to work and live here with your family."

Helen nodded. "I want you to ask me as many questions as you wish."

Lukas reminded Helen of what had happened to his parents in the war. He also told her about his uncle. Neither he nor I, though, mentioned our recent visit with him or the story he'd told us.

"Timon and I know," Lukas said, "Agamemnon's warriors forced my mother and father and uncle and other people like them to go to Troy. We understand neither you nor Menelaus had anything to do with that. But we have some questions concerning other matters. Did you choose to elope with Paris, or did he abduct you? If you freely ran off with him, did you know you'd bring about a war?"

Helen addressed one of those questions without any hesitation. "Paris didn't abduct me. He wasn't the kind of person who could've done that."

Lukas closed his eyes as if he'd heard all the evidence he needed to convict Helen.

"But I didn't know," Helen said, "if I went with Paris to Troy, Greece would go to war with the Trojans. I thought it was highly unlikely Achilles, Odysseus, Ajax and the other Greek kings would agree to fight a war to bring me back to Sparta. Agamemnon wanted a war with Troy, but not because I went to Troy with Paris."

Lukas's eyes were wide open now. "Agamemnon wanted to fight a war with the Trojans even if you hadn't gone to Troy with Paris?"

Helen nodded. "Agamemnon used my presence in Troy as an excuse to start a war. I was surprised when I learned the other Greek kings had agreed with him. I'd wrongly assumed they had far more sense than that."

"But you knew," Lukas said, "you were taking a chance the other Greek kings would go along with Agamemnon?"

Helen shook her head. "No, I wasn't taking a chance on anything. There's a lot more to my story from those days than the answers to your questions."

"I've always imagined there would be," I said.

"But I'm glad to know what your questions are," Helen said. "You deserve to have the answers to them. I invited you here to tell you what happened before I left Sparta and went to Troy with Paris. I want to tell you my story in full."

Lukas and I glanced at one another. Neither of us had anticipated this.

I could tell by the look on her face Helen had noticed our surprise. "Would you like to hear my story?"

"I would," I replied. "I very much would."

"So would I," Lukas said.

Helen

In my earliest memories in the orphanage, Clytemnestra and I remained at all times within an arm's length of one another. Solitary girls and boys were much more likely to suffer the theft of their food, a beating or other abuse by the orphans willing to take a chance on a beating of their own at the hands of a sharp-eyed guardian who might catch them misbehaving.

Clytemnestra never let down her guard. She was seven, I was six, and we were seated at a table in the orphanage dining room ready to consume our meal. She spotted an older boy reaching for my bowl of food from behind me.

"Thief!" she yelled.

The boy pulled back his hand and began slinking away, but that wasn't enough for Clytemnestra. Wielding the knife she ate her food with, she rose to her feet, ran after the boy like a wolf chasing a fawn, caught one of his flailing arms, turned him around and stabbed him in his belly through his tunic.

As the frightened boy wailed, Clytemnestra wiped his blood off her knife on his tunic, sat down next to me, cleaned her knife a second time with a napkin, and began eating her meal as if nothing at all out of the ordinary had happened.

The bleeding boy complained to the nearest guardian, whose name was Leda. She pulled up the boy's tunic, looked at his superficial wound and laughed.

"You'd better not try to steal food from those girls again," she told him, nodding toward Clytemnestra and me. "Next time, you might end up dead."

Helen

In those days, the guardians didn't merely ask the children to spend part of their time doing something useful. Work was a requirement for obtaining one's next meal. The guardians called it the no-work, no-food rule, and they strictly enforced it.

The work the guardians required us to perform wasn't intended to better enable us to find employment when we turned eighteen and left the orphanage. The work was routine and mindless for a good reason. The more so it was, the more easily the guardians could measure it and make certain we'd earned our meals. All they had to do was count the kitchen and dining room utensils and bowls we washed and dried, the pieces of clothing and bedding we laundered and hung out to dry on the lines, the fruits and vegetables we picked and brought to the kitchen, the garden rows we winnowed and weeded, the baskets of wheat and barley we cut and threshed.

Orphans who claimed to be too ill to work had to vomit frequently, be so feverish their skin was hot to the touch, or suffer dizziness of such severity they couldn't remain standing. Orphans who attempted to fake their symptoms ate no food for the next three days—unless their friends, if they had any, took pity on them, or they could find a way to steal it without getting beaten by a watchful guardian or stabbed to death by an angry older sister.

Then, too, even we orphans knew well more than half of us would die before we left the orphanage. Those who didn't make it out—either by running away early or walking away when we turned eighteen—were buried under the trees in the orchards and groves. The older orphans did that work, after the sun went down, using the light of torches or the moon.

Timon

"Is the Leda you mentioned," I asked Helen, "the same Leda who accompanies you to the orphanage sometimes?"

Whenever Menelaus and Hermione came with Helen, so did the woman named Leda.

My question seemed to please Helen. "She's the same Leda. When I came home from Troy, Menelaus and I asked her to live with us here. She accepted our invitation. She's picking berries today. She'll sell some of them to the people who can afford to buy them. She'll give the rest of them to those who can't. She told me she'd like to see you both after she's finished her work. I have to warn you, though. She'll probably ask you to sing for her."

"We'd love to sing for her," I said.

Lukas, though, stared at Helen as if he'd never seen her before.

"I'm very grateful to you," he said, "for making the orphanage a far more humane place than it was when you and your sister lived there. All of us who've lived in it since you became queen should be thankful for what you've done."

"I didn't feel I had any choice," Helen said. "When I came home from Troy and married Menelaus, he asked me to take charge of the orphanage. He understood a large number of the children living in it would be orphans of the war. But whoever they were, I'd never allow the guardians to continue mistreating them. And I promised the guardians I'd make their lives easier as well if they were kind to the children."

"You've accomplished what you set out to do," Lukas said.

Helen's Orphans

Helen

Clytemnestra and I were among the fortunate minority of the orphans who could and did perform the work the guardians expected of us. Due to the skimpy meals they fed the orphans, we were always hungry. Clytemnestra and I, though, never missed a meal. And we somehow survived our illnesses.

Leda befriended us. She was the only person resembling a parent we ever had. She taught us how to read and write and do arithmetic. She even introduced us to history, philosophy, poetry, geometry, botany, zoology, biology and astronomy.

I often wondered how Leda had learned what she knew. Then one day when she and I were alone weeding in one of the orphanage gardens, I asked her who her teacher was.

"I taught myself," she replied.

I separated a handful of weeds from their roots, threw them on the ground at my feet and turned to her.

"How did you do that?" I asked. "You would've had to have access to a library to teach yourself what you know."

She laughed. "I had access to a library."

I shook my head. "Only kings and queens have libraries."

She laughed again. "I had access to the library of a king and queen."

Helen

Menelaus, who was then seventeen years old, had taken to riding in his chariot on a path crossing the orphanage grounds. During one of his excursions, he saw Clytemnestra and me gathering fallen walnuts, which was our task for the day. After passing us a short distance, he turned his horse and chariot about and rode to the grove where we were working.

Staring at me, he stopped his horse and nodded toward the baskets we'd already filled with walnuts.

"The guardians must be pleased," he said, "you're working so hard."

Clytemnestra scoffed. "We're not doing this to please the guardians."

The remark brought a puzzled expression to our visitor's face.

"If we didn't fill these baskets," Clytemnestra said, "we wouldn't eat supper tonight."

77

Menelaus frowned. "You have to work, or you don't get fed?"

Clytemnestra laughed. "That's the rule in this orphanage."

Menelaus seemed surprised.

Clytemnestra laughed again. "They call it the no-work, no-food rule."

We and the other orphans had assumed Menelaus's family was wealthy. Very few Spartan boys went riding through the countryside on a chariot.

"What's your name?" Clytemnestra asked him.

"Menelaus," he replied.

Clytemnestra and I looked at one another without making any attempt to conceal our astonishment. The father of Menelaus, Atreus, had been the king of Sparta and Mycenae. He'd died earlier that year. He left the kingdom of Mycenae to his eighteen-year-old son Agamemnon. He left Sparta to Menelaus.

"You're the king," I said.

Menelaus chortled. "People tell me I'm the king."

He was, but he couldn't exercise the king's powers until he turned eighteen. In the meantime, a council of regents ruled Sparta for him.

Timon

"Did you find Menelaus attractive?" Lukas wanted to know.

I never would've asked Helen that question.

But it didn't seem to bother her. "I found him very attractive. He trained daily with the few warriors the regents had let him keep in the Spartan army."

Helen looked both Lukas and me up and down.

"He had a sinewy, muscular body like yours," she said. "He had close-set eyes and dark hair down to his shoulders. I found him very attractive."

Lukas and I had agreed Menelaus was still, two decades later, a pleasure to see. That raised, for us at least, another question. Had Paris been, twenty years ago, even more inviting?

Helen

Helen's Orphans

Clytemnestra had her own question for Menelaus in the walnut grove. "Do the regents at least let you hire people who work at the palace?"

He shrugged. "I haven't hired anybody yet, but maybe they'd let me do that. Do you have someone in mind I should hire?"

"You should hire me," Clytemnestra replied. "I'm quite skilled at doing many things. The guardians here will confirm that if you want."

"My sister is almost eighteen," I said. "She has to leave the orphanage soon. Everybody here thinks she's an excellent worker."

Menelaus was still looking at me. "Are you an excellent worker?" he asked.

"I'd say I'm a good worker," I replied. "My sister has taught me well."

"We're both damned good workers," Clytemnestra said.

"Would you like to work at the palace?" Menelaus asked me.

"I'd like to remain with my sister," I replied, "wherever she goes."

Menelaus nodded. "I'll ask the regents if I can hire two damned good workers for the palace. You'll have to do me a favor, though."

"What's that?" Clytemnestra asked.

For the first time since he'd stopped to speak with us, he looked at her. "Don't let anybody know I met you here."

"We'll never do that," Clytemnestra said. "This meeting will always be our secret."

He gave me one last look and rode off, this time toward the palace.

Ron Fritsch

Chapter Eleven

Helen

He knew this was the orphanage," Clytemnestra said, dropping a handful of walnuts into her basket. "He knew we were orphans. And I know why he was riding by here."

I laughed. "Did you know he was the king?"

"No, I never guessed that. I know what he wants, though."

"What's he want?"

"A pretty orphan girl like me in his bed. The kind of girl who's most unlikely to insist upon a marriage before she lies down with a handsome, young king in his bed."

I looked at Menelaus riding in his chariot in the distance. "Do you think he wants to share his bed with you?"

Clytemnestra laughed. "I have no doubt about it. And he'll do everything he can to make it happen. The regents will find out why he wants to hire two orphan sisters. You'll see."

Helen

We broke our promise to Menelaus and told Leda we wanted to work in the palace.

She begged us not to do that. "You'll live to regret it," she said.

"What do you mean?" I asked. "Don't people live well in palaces?"

Leda shook her head. "Not the people who work in them. The royal family and their favorites treat them like dirt. They live in tiny rooms in the basement."

Clytemnestra scoffed. "Then it's obvious we'll have to become favorites of the royal family as quickly as we can."

"You do that," Leda said, "and the next thing you know you'll be caught up in palace intrigues. Favorites today quickly become nobodies tomorrow—assuming they somehow manage to remain alive until tomorrow."

Clytemnestra laughed. "I'm not worried about remaining alive. Some people lose in this world. Other people win. You've told us yourself that's the way things are. And I intend to be a winner. I can guarantee you I'll never spend my life working in an orphanage."

If that remark hurt Leda, she didn't let it show.

Helen

In any event, Leda kept her promise not to let anybody else in the orphanage know what we intended to do until the day we left in a carriage Menelaus had sent for us.

"Goodbye to that horrible place," Clytemnestra said as we rode off, refusing to look back at the crowd of astonished guardians and orphans who'd just learned the destination of the two sisters found in a basket seventeen years ago.

I confess, though, I had more than a few tears in my eyes as I waved my farewell to Leda.

Helen

After we arrived at the palace, I asked to work in the royal stable.

Clytemnestra, though, chose to become a maid.

"You'll see," she told me. "I'll learn all the secrets here in no time at all. I'll go through this palace like a thief. But I won't be looking for precious jewels. No, I want information. It can be as good as gold. People will always do you favors to keep secret the bad things they've done."

Helen

My work brought me into daily contact with Menelaus, as I'd guessed it would. He soon decided I alone should look after his horse. I promised him the animal would receive my loving attention and care.

One afternoon he invited me to go riding in his chariot with him into the hills. We walked whenever the incline posed a burden for his horse. At the end of our ascent, we found a grassy area in the shade of a cypress where we could sit and talk and his horse could rest. The sea in the distance, which I'd never seen before, was like the sky turned upside down but a darker blue.

Helen's Orphans

He told me he no longer rode in his chariot on the path through the orphanage grounds.

"I did that," he said, "only because I wanted to meet you."

"You got your wish," I said, "the day my sister and I were gathering walnuts."

He laughed. "I'd seen you many times before. Until then, though, you were always too far away, or too many other people were around besides your sister, for us to speak privately."

I'd guessed, better than Clytemnestra had, what he was doing. It was why I volunteered her and me for walnut gathering. The grove was near the path, and I knew we'd be working alone.

Helen

Menelaus regularly invited me to ride in his chariot with him. More often than not, we'd end up under the cypress in the hills. His horse liked munching on the grass there more than the oats and hay I fed her in the stable.

Menelaus told me he was eagerly awaiting his eighteenth birthday.

"You'll become the ruling king of Sparta," I said. "You should look forward to that."

He nodded. "That's the day I'll change the way things are done in Sparta."

"What will you change?"

"Everything."

"Everything?"

"The first thing I'll do, I'll put the people's tax receipts to much better use than the regents do. You and your sister saw how it was in that damned orphanage. My father chose to spend as little as he could on it. After he died, the regents agreed to spend even less. My father at least liked to use some of his silver and gold to build roads. He told me they helped the people take to market whatever they grew, raised or built, and that brought more silver and gold into the treasury. But the regents have decided the people don't need any more roads. Nor do they need the existing roads kept in good repair. The regents have done the same thing with our army. Since we live in peace with our neighbors, they tell me, we don't need an army anymore."

"What are the regents doing with the silver and gold? I haven't heard they've lowered the taxes the people pay."

Menelaus scoffed. "Hell, no. They'd never do that."

"So what are the regents doing with it?" I insisted.

"They're using it to enrich themselves."

My next question brought me closer to learning what was wrong in Sparta.

"Who appointed the regents?" I asked.

"My brother, Agamemnon."

"Does he know what the regents are doing with the Spartan treasury?"

"He knows."

"Doesn't he care?"

Menelaus scoffed again. "He told me it's none of my concern until I become the ruling king. Then I can do whatever I please. I intend to do that, too."

Timon

Our history instructor had enjoyed telling Lukas and me and our classmates the story of Atreus, the father of Menelaus and Agamemnon. He and his twin brother had an older half brother. First the half brother and then the twin brother died in their youth. After both of their deaths, the royal family told the people they'd accidentally fallen from high places.

Our history instructor laughed at that explanation for their shortened lives.

"They were *pushed* from high places," she said.

According to her, Atreus and his twin brother pushed their half brother off a cliff. The twins had made an agreement. After their father's death, Atreus would become the king of Mycenae, and his twin would become the king of Sparta. Then Atreus pushed his twin off another cliff. When their father died, Atreus became the king of both Mycenae and Sparta.

"Pushing your rivals to their deaths from high places," our history instructor told us, "is just as foolproof as poisoning them."

"Why is that?" I asked, making no effort to conceal my naiveté.

84

Helen's Orphans

Our instructor laughed again. "If nobody sees you put poison in your victim's wine or give him a carefully planned shove, how can anybody prove you murdered him? In both cases, there's a dead body and nothing more."

After Atreus became the king, though, and above the law, he bragged more than once, under the influence of the excessive amounts of wine he consumed, he'd given both of his brothers their fatal shoves.

"They were stupid enough to trust me not to do it," he said. "Which only proved I was the brother most qualified to rule both Mycenae and Sparta."

Lukas and I had no reason to doubt our history instructor was telling the truth about Atreus. Helen, who'd married one of his two sons and was now a member of the royal family herself, had appointed our instructor to her position.

Helen

Clytemnestra came out to the stable several afternoons and couldn't find me. The other servants who worked in the stable were loyal to Menelaus and consistently told her they had no idea where I was. Then, late one day, she spotted Menelaus and me riding down from the hills in his chariot.

She had a question for me as soon as she and I were alone again in our basement room in the palace. "How long has this been going on?"

I looked her in the eye, having decided the truth would be the best medicine for her.

"Since we came here from the orphanage," I replied.

She glared at me. "You've been trysting with Menelaus all that while? And behind my back, up in the hills where nobody could see what a cheap slut you've become?"

"I haven't been trysting with Menelaus. I've done nothing with him behind your back."

"You never told me you've been spending your time with the king I've hoped to marry."

"You know everything else the people in this palace are doing."

I hadn't told her about riding to the hills with Menelaus because I'd seen this outburst coming.

And Clytemnestra wasn't done. "Has he slipped his hand under your tunic?"

"He's made no attempt to do that."

"Oh, dear," Clytemnestra said, laughing, "you must be disappointed."

"Why would I be disappointed Menelaus has sense enough to know he shouldn't do that with a person he's not married to?"

"You've talked about marriage with him, have you?"

"No, we haven't talked about marriage. Why would he wish to marry me? He'll soon be the ruling king of Sparta. I recently left an orphanage to work in his stable. I imagine his wife will be a very lucky princess."

"So why do you and he ride up to the hills together?"

"I enjoy his company. I assume he enjoys mine. Do we need another reason to spend time together in the hills? We have a wonderful view of the sea up there."

Clytemnestra chose to mock me. "A wonderful view of the sea—you won't admit what should be obvious, even to you."

"What's that?"

"He isn't in love with you."

At that point, I believed he was, but I didn't want to argue with Clytemnestra about it.

"I'm glad," she said, "I found out what you're doing. It's time for me to make my move. I'll let him know I'm available. I doubt there's an eligible princess as beautiful as I am."

I nodded. "You should let him know you're available. If he likes you, he should forget about any princess he might've had in mind. He should marry you. I'll be proud to say the queen of Sparta is my sister."

Helen

Despite her lowly status as a maid, Clytemnestra went to the king's chamber and knocked on his door. Menelaus opened the door and told her he didn't need the service of a maid at that time. He wondered if she'd been sent to his chamber in error.

Clytemnestra told him she was making a personal visit.

Menelaus invited her into his chamber. One of the few warriors he had left in his army was with him. They'd been lifting weights and jumping ropes together as part of their training.

Helen's Orphans

The warrior asked if he should leave, but Menelaus said he should stay. They'd worked long and hard enough, he said, to rest for a while and drink at least a small amount of wine. They could share their wine with their unexpected guest—who was, he explained to his warrior friend, "Helen's sister."

Helen

"That must've been a letdown," I said.

Clytemnestra had returned to our room and told me what had happened in the king's chamber.

"What do you think must've been a letdown?" she asked.

"Didn't you want to be with Menelaus alone?"

"Not at all. I was glad his friend was with us. He was proof Menelaus didn't think I was some foolish orphan girl who'd come to offer herself up to him in his bed. No, he treated me in his chamber as I'd wanted to be treated, as a marriage prospect—unlike yourself, I'm sorry to say. You might be a cheap afternoon tryst under a cypress in the hills with a lovely view of the sea, but you'll never be anything more than that."

"I haven't trysted with Menelaus."

Clytemnestra tittered. "You're clever not to admit it."

I took a deep breath. "Do you think Menelaus might want to marry you?"

"I have no doubt about it."

"Did you and he discuss what he hopes to accomplish after he becomes the ruling king?"

Clytemnestra scoffed. "Why would we wish to bore ourselves with that kind of talk? No, he and I spent our time together talking about nothing, looking into one another's eyes—the way lovers do."

Or, I thought to myself, the way people sizing one another up do.

"Should I prepare," I asked, "to play my part as your maid of honor?"

Clytemnestra looked at me and laughed. "You'd have the nerve to play a maid of honor after what you've done with the groom?"

Ron Fritsch

Chapter Twelve

Helen

Menelaus and I rode to our favorite spot in the hills the next afternoon. As soon as we sat down, I chose to mention my sister. "She told me she intruded on you in your chamber last night."

Menelaus laughed. "I wouldn't call her visit an intrusion. I assumed she came to see me because she's your sister."

I shook my head. "I doubt her being my sister had anything to do with her visit. She wants to marry you. Didn't she tell you that?"

Menelaus laughed again. "She made no mention to me of any desire for a marriage. If she had, I would've told her that's never going to happen."

I felt certain he would've done that.

He sat cross-legged next to me. I noticed the prominent bulge in his groin area I'd seen before during our chats under the cypress. Leda had explained to me what caused that when I'd observed it under the tunics of older boys in the orphanage.

"You've heard me talk a lot," Menelaus said, "about what I want to do when I become eighteen and say goodbye to the regents."

"I've heard you, and I don't doubt all Spartans, rich and poor alike, will be pleased with what you plan to do."

"But I'll have to do things step by step. I can't just issue a hundred orders the day I become an adult."

"I'm certain you're right about that. You've got to let the people sense where you and they are headed. Nobody wants to take a giant leap into the unknown."

"But I've changed my mind about the first important thing I'll do when I become the ruling king of Sparta. And I think the people will love me for doing it."

"Can you let me know what that first thing will be?"

"I have to let you, of all people, know."

His bulge was as large as I'd ever seen it.

"I want to marry you," he said. "I want you to be the queen of Sparta. I want you and me to lead Sparta together. I don't want to do it without you."

Timon

"That was the day," I asked Helen, "you agreed to marry Menelaus?"

Helen nodded. "That was the day. We sealed our agreement with our first kiss. I told him I very much looked forward to our wedding night."

"You freely agreed to marry Menelaus?" I asked.

Helen nodded again. "I didn't have to think about it. I wanted to marry him."

In one of the stories the people told, Helen had no desire to marry Menelaus. In some versions of that story, he'd won her in a game of chance he'd played with other Greek kings after they'd agreed she was the most beautiful woman in the world. One of the losing kings was his brother Agamemnon.

Lukas made no attempt to conceal his confusion.

"You were in love with Menelaus?" he asked.

"Very much so," Helen replied. "I've never not been in love with him since the day I met him in the orphanage walnut grove."

Helen

As soon as Clytemnestra and I returned to our room after our supper with the other palace workers that evening, I told her I'd agreed to marry Menelaus.

She looked at me as if I'd lashed her with a whip. "He asked you to marry him? Why does he need to marry you? He already gets what he wants from you."

"He wants me to help him rule Sparta when he turns eighteen."

"He wants you, a pitiful orphan girl, to help him rule Sparta? Has he taken leave of his senses?"

"I'll sit next to him as his queen. He thinks I'll be helpful to him."

Clytemnestra laughed. "He'll never marry you. He'll toss you aside when he's had his fill of you. Don't you remember what Leda told us? Men will promise marriage to get what they want. But after they've gotten what they want, they deny making any promises to get it."

Helen's Orphans

I decided it was my turn to laugh. "Menelaus and I have agreed he won't get what he wants from me—and I won't get what I want from him—until our wedding night. When we're together, at long last, in our bed. With our hastily removed clothes lying on the floor next to it."

Clytemnestra looked at me as if I'd given her another painful lash, even as if she thought I'd enjoyed doing it. I have to admit telling her what I did brought me no sorrow.

Helen

I no longer had to share a room in the basement of the palace with Clytemnestra. After Menelaus announced I was his bride-to-be, I was entitled to occupy the queen's chamber, which was next to his.

Clytemnestra, though, wasn't ready to give up her own pursuit of the king. Having figured out when he walked from the palace to the stable almost every day, she waited for him behind a row of bushes bordering the path he took. When he reached her hiding place, she emerged from it and confronted him.

"I'd like to ride with you to the hills today," she said.

She didn't know I'd taken a position behind the row of bushes on the other side of the path and could hear every word she said. I'd seen her lurking, and I'd correctly guessed why she was doing it.

Menelaus shook his head. "I intend to ride to the hills with your sister today."

Clytemnestra scoffed. "You can leave her here this afternoon. I'm sure she has a lot of work to do in the stable."

Menelaus shook his head again. "She only works in the stable now to help me take care of my horse. Didn't she tell you she and I plan to marry after I reach my eighteenth birthday?"

"She told me that. I think you're making a very big mistake, though."

"How am I making a mistake? I'm in love with her. She tells me she's in love with me. I believe she's saying that honestly."

"You won't be in love with her after you get to know her. For one thing, she isn't in love with you. She's in love with what you can do for her. You can take her from an orphanage and place her on the throne next to you. That's what she's in love with. You'll figure that out for yourself—before your marriage, I hope, rather than after you're married and the knowledge can no longer keep you from making a grievous mistake."

Menelaus looked at Clytemnestra as if she'd threatened to murder him.

"I'm surprised," he said, "you're so disloyal to your sister."

"I'm telling you what I know about Helen for your own good. Besides, she and I aren't sisters."

"You're not? She told me the orphanage guardians found you and her in the same basket."

"They found us in the same basket, but they also discovered I was a royal child, and she was a child of working people. She was left in the basket with me to become my servant. I should have a chamber in your palace. She should be my maid and live in the basement with the other servants."

Menelaus seemed confused. "How did the orphanage guardians know you were a royal child? How did they know Helen was the child of servants?"

Through the leaves of the bushes, I could see how much Clytemnestra enjoyed the game she was playing.

"Somebody," she replied, "had embroidered our names in our tunics. Whoever did it had used blue thread for mine—the blue of the sky and the sea, royal blue. And green thread for Helen's—the green of the earth, of the fields and orchards, of working and taking orders from one's betters."

Whoever had sewn our names and birth dates in our tunics had in fact used blue thread for Clytemnestra's and green for mine. But none of the guardians had agreed with her on what those colors meant. Leda said the sewer had obviously chosen those colors at random.

Clytemnestra had an answer to that reasonable view of the matter. She told me the guardians, especially Leda, had denied the colors of the threads meant anything because they favored me and didn't wish to hurt my feelings.

Clytemnestra looked at Menelaus and laughed. "If you want a royal wife," she said, "you'll choose me. If you want a daughter of servants for your wife, you'll choose Helen."

Menelaus took no time at all to consider his response to those remarks. "I don't give a damn who your or Helen's parents were. I've chosen Helen for my wife. And to be very honest, I'd never choose you."

He turned away from Clytemnestra and resumed his walk to the stable to prepare for his ride into the hills with me that afternoon.

Helen

Agamemnon chose to celebrate his nineteenth birthday in Sparta. He wished to do so, he gave as his excuse, because he'd grown up in the Spartan palace. As Menelaus's betrothed, I was expected to attend the festivities in honor of the king of Mycenae.

So was Clytemnestra, as my sister, whether she wished to acknowledge she and I were related or not. Despite the harsh words she and Menelaus had exchanged on the path to the stable, he'd prevailed upon the regents to raise her, again as my sister, from her servant's room in the basement to the upper-floor chamber next to mine.

During the evening of the day she moved into her new quarters, she knocked on my door and asked if we could chat for a while.

I invited her in. We sat side by side on chairs in my front room.

She soon revealed why she'd decided to pay me a visit.

"Agamemnon is looking for a wife," she said. "That's why he's coming to Sparta."

Menelaus had told me his brother was unmarried and shared his bed with a servant he had no wish to marry.

Clytemnestra wasn't about to end her story with a mere hint. "You've found yourself a king to marry," she said. "I can't see why I shouldn't be able to do what you've done."

"Do you have Agamemnon in mind as the king you might wish to marry?"

Clytemnestra nodded. "It wouldn't be the first time two sisters married two brothers."

"You haven't met him yet."

"Why should that matter? He's the perfect age for me. He's coming here to celebrate his nineteenth birthday. I haven't heard anybody say he can't do what a husband is supposed to do in bed. Better yet, he's a king. Best of all, he's a ruling king with an army and a treasury only he controls. He doesn't have regents standing in his way. Why would I need to meet such a person before I decided I wanted to marry him?"

93

"I'd imagine others might feel the way you do."

"But how many of those others are as beautiful as I am?"

I honestly agreed with Clytemnestra on that point.

"Probably very few," I replied, "if any at all. But we have no way to know whether Agamemnon will agree with us."

"I have no doubt he will."

"Then you have nothing to worry about. You'll marry a king."

"And you won't stand in my way?"

"Why would I wish to stand in your way—even if I could?"

"You wouldn't be upset I'd found my own king to marry?"

I shook my head and laughed. "You deserve a king for a husband. You shouldn't settle for anybody who isn't a king. Not if a king is what you want."

Helen

I stood with Menelaus and the regents and their spouses and companions in the first line outside the front entrance to the palace. We were there to greet Agamemnon upon his arrival. Wearing his diadem, which was a thin gold headband, and carrying his scepter, an olivewood staff taller than he was, he stepped down from his carriage.

As protocol required, he proceeded from regent to regent, acknowledging by name and chatting with each of the elderly men he'd appointed to serve as protectors of the interests of his brother and Sparta. Every chance he got, though, he turned away from the tedious, ceremonial business at hand and looked down the line at me.

Agamemnon was a taller and brawnier version of his brother Menelaus, but he carried with him so much presumption and so little humility I suspected from those first moments in his diademed and sceptered presence I wouldn't enjoy having him for a brother-in-law.

After he'd made his way along the line to a position in front of me, he looked me up and down as if he were in a market and I were for sale to the highest bidder.

"You are," he said, "what I've been told you are."

"And what might that be?" I asked, looking at the blue sky above his head, hoping I'd appear to be no more interested in his answer than if he'd offered to divulge his thoughts on the day's weather.

Helen's Orphans

He replied to my question without making any effort to limit the volume of his voice.

"You are," he said, laying the basis for the stories bandied about later, "the most beautiful woman in the world."

Clytemnestra stood somewhere behind those of us in the first line of greeters. After Agamemnon finished his remark, I could hear her gasp.

Ron Fritsch

Chapter Thirteen

Helen

During his birthday celebration in the great hall in the Spartan palace that evening, Agamemnon approached me. He held a cup of wine in his hand in place of his scepter.

"I wish to meet with you alone," he whispered in my ear.

"I'll enjoy meeting with you alone," I said, making certain my voice was loud enough for Menelaus to hear me. "You must have any number of naughty boyhood stories you can tell me about my husband-to-be. I look forward to hearing them all."

The look on Agamemnon's face let me know he had no desire to tell me boyhood stories, naughty or not.

I decided that wouldn't stop me. "There's one big question I'll have for you," I said.

"What will that be?" Agamemnon asked.

"Why didn't your father leave you both of his kingdoms? You were his older son. Why did he leave one of his kingdoms to his younger son?"

Agamemnon looked at me as if I'd punched him in his gut.

Even though many Greeks were asking those same questions, I'd assumed he wouldn't want to hear them from me.

"When you're ready to leave your birthday celebration," I said, again making certain Menelaus could hear me, "we can go to my chamber. We can talk the night away there."

Menelaus wasn't the only person listening to my conversation with his brother. So was Clytemnestra.

Timon

Helen could tell Lukas and I were more than a little concerned at this point in her story. Our history instructor at the orphanage had emphasized Agamemnon's cruelty. During the war, she told us, he'd raped a number of the Trojan women his warriors had taken prisoner.

"Weren't you worried," I asked, "Agamemnon would attack you in your chamber?"

Helen laughed. "Not at all. Menelaus sent two of his most trustworthy warriors to accompany his brother and me to my chamber. And along the way to our destination, they let Agamemnon know they'd remain outside the door to my chamber as long as he was there."

"Did they have a key to open the door and rush in," Lukas asked, "if they'd heard you scream?"

Helen laughed again. "They had a key to open the door and rush in," she said, "if they'd heard Agamemnon scream."

Helen

Without waiting for an invitation to do so, Agamemnon sat down on one of my chairs in my front room. I chose for myself a chair opposite the one he'd selected, the better for us to talk, I thought, eye to eye.

"You're lucky," he said.

"I'm lucky?" I asked. "How do you arrive at that conclusion?"

"I've found you," he replied, "before you married my brother."

He sat in his chair as stiff and regal as he had in his carriage when he'd arrived at the palace that day. I felt somewhat disappointed he hadn't brought his diadem and scepter with him to my chamber.

I shook my head. "I still don't understand what you're attempting to say. How does your finding me before my marriage to your brother make me lucky?"

Agamemnon knew I was playing him. "You're still free," he said.

"Free to do what?"

"You're free to break off your engagement to that worthless, pretty-boy brother of mine and marry me."

"Why on earth would I wish to do that?"

Agamemnon didn't seem displeased I was making our conversation a game. I suspected he thought it was a game he'd win in any event.

"I'm a king," he said, "with a substantial treasury and a powerful army."

"So I've heard."

"I'm the first son of Atreus. I'm the inevitable leader of all the Greeks."

"Have the other Greek kings acknowledged you as their leader?"

Agamemnon glowered. "They will. I'll leave them no choice."

"Achilles, Odysseus and Ajax will have no other choice?"

98

Helen's Orphans

"Not even Achilles, Odysseus and Ajax. They'll have no choice at all. When the time comes, they'll appear to be boys taking directions from their father—and not daring to disobey."

Achilles and Odysseus were still young men, but they and all the other Greek kings, except Menelaus, were older than Agamemnon. Ajax was a generation older.

"So let's assume," I said, "you become the leader of all the Greeks. Why should that entice me to break my engagement to your brother and marry you?"

Agamemnon looked at me as if he wondered how much longer the game would take. "Don't you think the most powerful man in the world deserves to have the most beautiful woman in the world at his side—to show the people she's his? Don't you think the most beautiful woman in the world deserves to stand next to the most powerful man in the world?"

I couldn't help but notice in Agamemnon's formulation the most powerful man would *have* the most beautiful woman and show the people she was *his*, but the most beautiful woman would merely *stand next to* the most powerful man.

"Suppose," I said, "I am the most beautiful woman in the world. How long will that last? Suppose, as well, you become the most powerful man in the world. How long will that last?"

"Beauty might not last as long as we wish it would. Power, though, can last at least as long as one's lifetime."

"So why should I buy what you're offering me? My beauty will be gone, but you'll still have your power."

"Living in comfort for the rest of your life as the queen of the most powerful man in the world isn't enough for you? Didn't my brother recently rescue you from an orphanage?"

"I'm grateful he brought me to his palace. He's the kindest man I've ever met."

"That's nice, but you need to set your sights higher than *his* palace."

"Which would be *your* palace?"

"Which would be *my* palace."

"I can't do that. I'm in love with your brother. I only wish to live with him in his palace. As long as he's alive, I'll have no chance for happiness living with anyone else."

Agamemnon scoffed. "He'll never be the king I am. If you choose to live with him, you'll be giving up a lot."

I laughed. "I'd live with Menelaus if he were a shepherd. I'd live with him if he were a shepherd with no land of his own. I'd live with him if he were a shepherd who tended other people's sheep and goats."

Agamemnon curled his upper lip. "An impoverished shepherd is about what you'll get if you marry Menelaus."

"I'd hardly call the king of Sparta an impoverished shepherd."

"I'll make the king of Sparta an impoverished shepherd if you marry him."

"You can do whatever you please. I'll still marry him."

I could tell from the look on Agamemnon's face he wasn't used to defiance.

"Even if I weren't in love with Menelaus," I chose to add, "I'd never marry you."

"You don't know who you're saying that to."

"I know perfectly well who I'm saying that to. You're a thug who uses threats to get what he wants. To be honest, I find it hard to believe you and Menelaus are brothers. Maybe, at some point, say nine months before Menelaus was born, your mother shared a bed with a man who wasn't your father? A man who was far more kind and gentle than fratricidal Atreus?"

Agamemnon scowled. "The most beautiful woman in the world might live to regret she has such a nasty mouth."

I stood up, went to the door to my chamber, opened it and turned to Agamemnon.

"I've heard enough from you," I said. "It's time for you to leave."

Helen

Soon after Agamemnon left my chamber, Clytemnestra came to see me.

"Has he changed your mind?" she asked. "Have you agreed to marry him?"

"No," I said, "I haven't changed my mind."

We remained standing in the front room of my chamber. The windows were open. In the moonlight I could see the hills Menelaus and I had spent a number of afternoons in.

Clytemnestra had more questions for me. "Did he ask you to marry him?"

"He did."

"And you turned him down?"

"I turned him down. I told him Menelaus is the only man I wish to marry."

Clytemnestra looked as pleased as a child receiving a birthday gift far beyond her expectations.

"I'll have to let him know I'm available," she said. "That might change his mind about which of us is the most beautiful woman in the world."

I suspected it might have the opposite effect, but I once again chose not to argue a point with my sister.

"You're a far more beautiful person," I said, "than Agamemnon deserves. After talking with him, I'm certain all those stories we've heard about him are true. He's incapable of loving any person the way you should be loved. I hope, for your sake, he doesn't want to marry you."

Clytemnestra shook her head. "You say that because you don't want me to marry a king. Why don't you admit it? You want to marry a king and become a queen, but you don't want me to be anything more than a queen's poor sister. You'd love to see me picking among the servants for a husband."

I confess, up to that point, I'd never considered viewing such matters the way Clytemnestra did. I'd never hoped to be a queen or anybody else important in the world. I only wanted to be a queen then because that's what I'd become after Menelaus and I married and began sharing a bed. And if Menelaus had preferred Clytemnestra to me, as she'd hoped, I would've been happy for her. I would've been pleased, too, if I could've found someone among the servants to love as much as I did Menelaus.

Helen

Clytemnestra knocked on my door again after she returned from her meeting with Agamemnon.

As soon as she closed the door behind her, she wagged an index finger in my face. "You made it damned difficult for me even to speak with him. He said he'd heard enough insults from you to totally ruin his nineteenth-birthday celebration. And why should he expect to hear anything more pleasing from me?"

"So you weren't able to let him know you're eager to become his bride?"

Clytemnestra laughed. "Don't you wish! No, I had to stand my ground and disavow any allegiance to you."

I'd heard her do that before.

"I got my message through to him," she continued. "It wasn't long before he was looking me up and down the way men do, imagining what they'll see when the clothes come off."

"I hope you didn't remove your clothes for him."

Clytemnestra rolled her eyes. "A would-be queen doesn't remove her clothes, even for a king—not until she becomes the queen. Then she lets him rip them off her, if that's what he wants to do. Why should she care? He pays the bills to replace them."

I wondered then if I should've previously noticed how cynical my sister had become. I'd heard other people in the palace speaking the way she did, but I hadn't thought we'd lived there long enough to indulge in that kind of talk ourselves.

"Did he go beyond looking you up and down?" I asked. "Did he give you any reason to hope he might accept your marriage proposal?"

"You won't like my answer, but yes, he did. He told me he'd seriously consider my candidacy for the position of his queen. He even said I should be sure to tell you that. He's going home as soon as he can tomorrow morning, thanks to you. And if you wish to reconsider the unkind remarks you made to him, you know where to reach him."

I laughed. "You won't need to worry about that. I'll never take back what I said to him."

Timon

Lukas had a question for Helen. "Did Clytemnestra tell Agamemnon about the blue and green threading in your tunics when the orphanage guardians found you?"

Helen chuckled. "She made sure he knew she was royalty, and I wasn't."

"What was Agamemnon's reaction to that?" Lukas asked.

Helen's Orphans

"He said he wasn't surprised. From the moment he'd met me, in the receiving line, he thought I was an ignorant servant."

Lukas shook his head. "But your seeming to be an ignorant servant hadn't stopped him from calling you the most beautiful woman in the world."

Helen laughed. "I'm certain Agamemnon didn't care how ignorant I might've been. He told me I was the most beautiful woman in the world to get my attention. He no doubt thought I'd be grateful for that kind of meaningless flattery. Whoever I was, and however beautiful I was, or wasn't, Agamemnon wanted me because I'd fallen in love with his brother."

Ron Fritsch

Chapter Fourteen

Helen

Agamemnon sent a messenger to Clytemnestra with an invitation to visit him at his palace. She decided, on the spot, to pack all of her belongings and go to Mycenae in the messenger's carriage. She had no doubt Agamemnon would ask her to marry him.

"There's no need for any further delay," she told me. "I'm sure he has a chamber prepared for me to live in before our wedding day."

She sat in the carriage waiting for the servants to finish bringing her possessions down from her chamber.

"I'll accept his proposal as soon as he makes it," she said. "You could've been the wife of the most powerful king in Greece. But no, being the foolish and stubborn girl you've always been, you turned him down. So you'll lose the greatest prize of them all, and I'll win him."

Helen

Clytemnestra returned to Sparta five days later.

"Did Agamemnon ask you to marry him?" I inquired as soon as I saw her again, which was in the corridor outside our chambers.

She was shouting at the servants, instructing them where to put her possessions. She wanted all of them precisely where they'd been before she'd left for Mycenae.

"If you must know," she said, turning to me, "I wasn't anticipating a proposal from him during my first visit to his palace. He made certain, though, I was entertained from the moment I arrived to the moment I left. He took me to see all the beautiful sights his land has to offer."

"I hope," I said, "those sights didn't include him lying naked on his bed."

Clytemnestra laughed. "Those sights could've included that. He asked me, more than once, if I wished to join him in his bed. I made it clear to him, though, I'm not prepared to do that with any man until the night of the day I marry him."

Ron Fritsch

Helen

Menelaus had spoken with the carriage driver who'd brought Clytemnestra home. He'd been a warrior in the Spartan army before the regents decided there was no further need for one. He and many of his comrades had joined the Mycenean army.

From their conversation, Menelaus concluded his brother had an underhanded reason to invite Clytemnestra to his palace.

"He wanted to provoke you," Menelaus told me.

"Provoke me?"

We were in the hills sitting on the grass beneath our cypress.

Menelaus nodded. "He wanted to provoke you into letting him know you'd be open to an invitation of your own to his palace."

I shook my head. "I'll accept an invitation to your brother's palace only if it includes you—and you think we have a damned good reason to accept it."

Helen

Menelaus and I soon received an invitation to his brother's palace. And it included a reason for us to accept it. Agamemnon asked us to attend his wedding.

The regents and other wealthy citizens in Sparta also received invitations. Neither theirs nor ours, though, disclosed who the bride would be.

Clytemnestra's at least included a hint. She showed it to me in her chamber. The servants were once again packing all of her belongings.

Agamemnon had included a question in her invitation. "Do you still wish to be my wife and queen?"

"He's invited people to his wedding," I said, "without having an agreement yet to marry anyone."

Menelaus had learned his brother had invited all the other kings of Greece as well, including Achilles, Odysseus and Ajax.

"With a guest list like that," Clytemnestra said, "he'll have to marry somebody."

She went to give a servant specific instructions on how she wanted her undergarments packed. Then she returned to me and removed her invitation from my hand.

Helen's Orphans

"Now all we need to do," she said, "is to find out which lucky person will become his bride. Maybe, if I turn him down, he'll have a few maids available to choose from."

"But you don't intend to turn him down, do you?"

"Of course not. This will be the most talked-about wedding of our time. Your wedding won't get nearly as much attention as mine does. Achilles, Odysseus and Ajax will send distant cousins, if they send anybody at all, to yours."

Helen

When we arrived at Agamemnon's palace, we learned Clytemnestra had correctly anticipated the Greek kings would attend the wedding themselves and not send proxies. A huge crowd of Myceneans, helping themselves to Agamemnon's wine and food, gathered outside the entrance to the palace to watch the kings and queens arrive.

When Menelaus, Clytemnestra and I stepped down from our carriage, a messenger approached me. "The king wishes to speak with you in his chamber," she said.

I shook my head. "I think you've made a mistake. I'm Helen. I believe you wish to deliver your message to my sister Clytemnestra."

"No," the messenger said without glancing at Clytemnestra, who stood next to me listening to every word the messenger and I spoke. "The king wishes to see you."

I went with the messenger to Agamemnon's chamber. I asked her to wait for me in the corridor. She had a key to the chamber as well as a long dagger in a shield on her person.

She grimaced. "In case you need my assistance?"

I laughed. "In case the king needs your assistance."

Helen

"This is your last chance," Agamemnon said.

Once again, I chose to sit on a chair facing him.

"My last chance for what?" I asked.

"To agree to be my bride."

"I haven't changed my mind. I have no wish to be your wife."

"You're making a terrible mistake."

107

"I'm certain I'm not making a mistake. I wish to be your brother's wife and companion. I wish to share a bed with him. I wish to live with him for the rest of my life."

"You're a fool."

He and Clytemnestra were in agreement on that.

"Even if I weren't in love with Menelaus," I chose to add, "I wouldn't consider being your wife. Greece must have ten thousand servants and shepherds I'd choose over you. Not only for their physical beauty but also for their kindness—like your brother's."

Agamemnon scoffed. "You're a total fool. No servant or shepherd deserves beauty like yours. Only a great king deserves you."

"I'm engaged to be married to a great king."

Agamemnon laughed. "Menelaus will never be a great king. He has no ambition. That's what's wrong with him. Our father should've left both Mycenae and Sparta to me. He shouldn't have given Menelaus anything except the indifference a second son deserves."

"How do you intend to become a great king?"

"I'm going to lead the Greeks in a war against the Trojans. I'll win the war too."

"Why do the Greeks need to fight a war against the Trojans."

"They're interfering with our trading. We Greeks depend upon our trading. The Trojans are pirates. They stop our ships and steal our cargoes."

"I understand Greeks have also been known to stop Trojan ships and take their cargoes."

"We do it only in retaliation. If you've got an empty ship out in the middle of the sea, you need a cargo before you reach your destination. But the details of that business don't matter. My war will put an end to it. After my armies reduce Troy to rubble, Greek ships will sail all the seas without having to worry about Trojan pirates."

Menelaus had told me about his brother's obsession to unite the Greeks under his command, destroy the Trojans in an all-out war and go down in history as the greatest king and military commander the Greeks had ever known. Many Greeks, though, considered the occasional Trojan acts of piracy as more of a nuisance than a reason to fight a war. Greek traders had learned to work together, assemble flotillas of ships and provide extensive training for their sailors in defending their ships against pirates wherever they came from. The traders who chose to send a single ship out to sea with untrained sailors on it had to know the chances they were taking, even if the neophyte sailors who sometimes died on those ships didn't.

"Do the other Greek kings agree with you?" I asked. "Do they believe a war with the Trojans is necessary?"

Agamemnon tried to bluff his way past those questions. "They will," he replied.

"Achilles and Odysseus will fight a war with the Trojans under your command?"

"They will. But right now I need a wife. I need a wife whose beauty captures the attention of the Greek people."

"My sister Clytemnestra is the wife you need for that."

Agamemnon looked at me as if I were attempting to play him for a fool.

"Your sister isn't the beauty you are," he said. "You know that as well as I do."

I wondered if I'd still be the beauty he said I was if I hadn't previously refused to marry him—if I hadn't told him I was in love with his brother.

"You'll marry Clytemnestra anyway," I asked, "if I turn you down?"

"That's what I intend to do. I also intend to make you regret turning me down. Menelaus too. I'll make him feel as much pain as you will. This is your last chance to avoid that pain, for yourself and Menelaus."

I rose to my feet. "Consider yourself turned down for good. I'll never marry a person who dares to threaten me into it. If my sister Clytemnestra is willing to marry such a person, so be it. But I have no doubt she'll live to wish she hadn't."

Helen

Clytemnestra was waiting for me outside the door to the chamber I'd been assigned.

As soon as we entered the chamber, she went straight to what mattered the most to her. "Did you agree to marry him?"

"How did you know he'd ask me a second time to marry him?"

She looked at me with narrowed eyes. "All the servants here know that's why he sent for you. And all the other guests—all the kings and queens in Greece—know that by now too. But you haven't answered my question. Did you, or didn't you, agree to marry him?"

"He threatened he'd make Menelaus and me both regret my refusal to marry him."

"And you refused to marry him anyway?"

"Why need you ask? Of course I refused to marry him."

"Did he say anything about me?"

"He said he'd marry you if I turned him down again."

Clytemnestra seemed torn between joy and sorrow, like a visitor to a seashore on a sunny afternoon confronted with the sight of a ship sinking and taking all onboard to the bottom.

"Everybody will know," she said, "I was his second choice. They'll sit there at my wedding knowing that. They'll make every attempt not to laugh, especially when they're face-to-face with me, but some, inevitably, won't be able to resist the temptation. I'm sure I couldn't."

"Will you marry him anyway?"

"Without any hesitation whatsoever. My marriage to him will deny you your dearest wish."

"My dearest wish? What do you imagine that is?"

"To outrank me."

Helen

During my conversation with Agamemnon, Clytemnestra had paid a visit to Menelaus in his chamber. She renewed her proposal to marry him. She told him she'd be pleased to be his wife whether I agreed to marry Agamemnon or not.

She assured Menelaus he was her first choice. Agamemnon wasn't.

Menelaus told her he was certain I wouldn't agree to marry Agamemnon. But even if I did, he said, he still wouldn't wish to marry her.

Timon

Lukas had another question for Helen. "Did Clytemnestra explain to Menelaus why she preferred him to Agamemnon?"

Helen laughed. "My sister didn't leave that out. She told Menelaus she was certain she'd enjoy sharing his bed far more than she would Agamemnon's. She'd already admitted that to me."

"So Agamemnon was her second choice," I said, "just as much as she was his."

Helen nodded. "They were both settling for the other."

"Did Agamemnon know that?" I asked.

"He did," Helen replied. "I made sure he did. I told him. It was an unnecessary, mean thing for me to do, but I was young then and couldn't imagine the trouble lying ahead for all of us."

Ron Fritsch

Chapter Fifteen

Helen

In the wedding ceremony the next day, Menelaus, as the groom's only brother, and I, as the bride's only sister, had to play the parts tradition required of us. When I swore I was certain my sister loved Agamemnon and no other person, and would always remain loyal to him, the wedding guests, led by Achilles, Odysseus and the other Greek kings, openly laughed. When Menelaus swore he also had no doubt his brother loved Clytemnestra and no other person, and would always remain loyal to her, the wedding guests guffawed again as if we were characters in a bawdy farce.

Having heard the servants talk, Clytemnestra had predicted the merriment, but I doubt she'd anticipated how loud it would be. But if it bothered her, she didn't let it show. Neither did Agamemnon.

Helen

When the guests sat down to consume a meal during the festivities after the ceremony, first Achilles and Patroclus, and then Odysseus and Penelope, joined Menelaus and me at our table. They chose to sit with us even though Agamemnon had specifically invited them to sit at his and his new wife's table.

Helen

When I said goodbye to Clytemnestra in her chamber the next morning, she let me know what she thought about the snub.

"You were responsible for that," she said.

Like the wedding guests the day before, I couldn't help but laugh. "How was I, an orphan girl, responsible for what two great kings of Greece and their companions decided to do?"

"They wanted to be seen," she snapped, "with the most beautiful woman in the world. As a result, only pathetic lesser kings sat at our table. It was your doing."

"Menelaus and I should've turned those people away?"

"It would've been the right thing to do. After all, it was *my* wedding."

Helen

During the preparations for the celebration of Menelaus's eighteenth-birthday and the end of the regency in Sparta, he and I decided to invite not only the Greek kings and queens but the king and queen of Troy as well. We doubted elderly Priam and Hecuba would put in an appearance themselves, but we dared to hope they'd send their older son Hector in their place. Greek traders who visited Troy told a consistent story. Priam and Hecuba made no decision without consulting Hector first.

Then we learned they'd chosen to send Hector's younger brother Paris to represent them. The Greek traders knew who he was. Unlike Hector, he took no part in ruling Troy. Eighteen-year-old Paris had chosen instead to spend his time training for athletic competitions.

Menelaus and I rode to the harbor in his chariot one day and spoke with several traders who could give us information about the Trojan royal family. When Menelaus asked them how well Paris competed, they agreed he rarely lost.

"You mean," I asked, "his opponents know better than to attempt to beat a prince?"

The traders shook their heads.

"He tells all his opponents," one trader said, "he doesn't want them to let him win. He says if he suspects they're doing that, he'll publicly expose them."

"The Trojans love him," another trader said.

"Some people tell me," a third trader said, "Hector is jealous. The Trojans don't pay nearly as much attention to him as they do his brother. And Hector's word is law in Troy."

"Maybe Hector hopes," a fourth trader chose to say, "we Greeks will kill his brother."

"I can't imagine," I said, "the Trojan people would be happy if we killed their hero."

"They wouldn't," the fourth trader agreed. "But what could they do about it?"

As we rode back to the palace, Menelaus said he'd ask his warriors to keep an eye on Paris while he was in Sparta. "I don't think we Greeks want to commit a murder for Hector."

Helen's Orphans

Helen

We were at the harbor again when our guest from Troy disembarked from his ship. The three guards the regents had allowed him to bring with him carried spears and had swords and daggers in shields on their bodies.

The traders had told us the royal family of Troy and many other Trojans spoke Greek. We soon learned Paris, as well as his guards, spoke it fluently.

Paris accepted our invitation to share our carriage for the drive from the harbor to the palace. His guards rode behind us in the chariots they'd brought from Troy. Menelaus and I sat on the rear seat of our carriage. Paris sat on the front seat facing us.

"We understand," I said, "you're an athlete."

Paris nodded. "I enjoy competing in the games."

"We've been told," I said, "you win most of the games you compete in."

Paris grinned. "I have the advantage of being a prince."

His remark seemed contrary to what the traders had told us.

"What's your advantage?" I asked.

"Unlike most of my opponents," Paris replied, "I have as much time as I wish to train."

Menelaus nodded. "That's a big advantage."

"I'm glad you invited my father and mother to Greece," Paris said. "And I'm glad they decided to send me in their place. I've always wanted to come to Greece. But they and my brother told me I couldn't just show up here as a visitor. As a prince, I had to have an invitation to pay you a visit."

"Why have you wanted to visit Greece?" I asked.

"I can't imagine not wanting to come here. Your people are inventive and industrious. Your traders are welcome everywhere. You produce so many things other people want."

"Do other Trojans," I asked, "share your view of Greece?"

"Of course they do. Trojans might not be Greeks, but they aren't stupid. They see how things are. They want to be as much like Greeks as they can."

Why, I couldn't help wonder, would the Greek kings want to start a war with this young man's people?

115

"I have another reason for wanting to come to Greece," he said. "It's more personal."

"Can you tell us what it is?" I asked.

"I want to compete in your games. Everybody says Greece has the best athletes. That's why I want to compete against them."

"And if you won," I said, "your people would love you more than they already do."

Paris laughed. "They'd love hearing a Trojan competed against Greeks and won."

"What makes you think," Menelaus asked, "you can't compete in Greek games?"

Paris looked at Menelaus as if the question surprised him. "Your kings don't allow it. Trojan athletes have come to Greece to participate in your games, but they've been turned away. One of your kings said no Trojan will compete in a Greek game as long as he's alive."

"Which one of our kings said that?" Menelaus asked.

Paris frowned. "I was told he's your brother, Agamemnon."

Menelaus scowled as well. "He's my brother. I'll introduce you to him during the festivities. Maybe you can persuade him to let you and other Trojans compete with our athletes."

I looked at Menelaus and scoffed. "I doubt persuasion will change your brother's mind."

"My history tutor tells me," Paris said, "Greeks and Trojans used to compete against one another. There are all sorts of stories, she says, in which they did. Then, not so long ago, the Greek kings decided to keep the Trojans out of their games. She thinks they did it because they see us now less as neighbors they're happy to trade with and more as rivals they don't need."

"I think," I said, "your history tutor has got that right."

Paris nodded. "I'm glad my mother hired her. She's taught me everything I know about history. I love hearing her stories about our ancestors, Trojans and Greeks both, and how they struggled to understand the world. And we're still doing it today."

"I assume," I said, "you wouldn't want to see your people go to war with us Greeks."

"Absolutely not. A war with your people would be a disaster for the Trojans. We all know what would happen as soon as the war started.

Our so-called allies to the east would desert us. They'd let us fight the mighty Greeks on our own."

"What about your parents and brother?" Menelaus asked. "Do they wish to avoid a war with Greece?"

I could see Paris didn't care much for that question.

"My parents and my brother," he said, "avoid discussing things like that with me. They think I should stick to entertaining the crowds who come out to see me in the games. Hector knows I admire your people. But he tells me I shouldn't share my opinion on that with our people. He says a member of the royal family who speaks favorably of the Greeks is a traitor."

"A traitor?" I asked. "He'd go so far as to call you that?"

"My history instructor tells me she wouldn't be surprised if some Greeks wanted to fight a war with us. She says we're becoming too competitive with your people. Some of the traders from other lands are as willing to do business with our traders as they are with yours. Many of our crops are as plentiful as yours, and many of our crafts are as well-made. And our traders can sell a lot of those things for less than what the Greek traders want."

"And your instructor," Menelaus asked, "believes that could lead to a war?"

"She says economic competition has caused wars in the past. And nothing has changed in the world to prevent it from happening again."

In the long pause that followed those remarks in the carriage, I imagined the crowds who watched Paris compete in athletic games might've taken him to be an innocent youth, pushing himself to his limits to retain their favor. I could also see, though, he was much more than that.

Timon

Lukas had yet another question for Helen. I knew what this one would be, word for word, before he asked it.

"Did you find Paris attractive?"

Helen didn't hesitate. "He was a champion runner and wrestler. The tunic he wore that summer day didn't hide his muscular body. I thought he was extremely attractive. I would've been very happy for anybody he fell in love with."

And, as I'd also anticipated, nosy Lukas couldn't let the matter rest there.

"Did you find him more attractive than Menelaus?"

Helen gave no indication she found the question as uncalled-for as I did.

She shook her head. "I couldn't imagine finding either of them more attractive than the other. I thought at the time how fortunate I was to be riding in a carriage on a lovely afternoon in Sparta with two paragons of youthful male beauty."

She glanced at me, returned her gaze to Lukas and beamed.

"Now I'm in the royal olive grove on a lovely afternoon in Sparta in a very similar situation. I needed an artist then to capture the moment. I could use one again today. The images would come to be known as Helen in the royal carriage with Menelaus and Paris, and Helen in the royal olive grove with Lukas and Timon."

Whatever the precise details of Helen's story were, she knew, since her retrieval from Troy had been the excuse for one of the most senseless wars fought, she'd never be forgotten.

Helen

When we returned to the palace, Paris accepted Menelaus's invitation to stay in his chamber during his visit to Sparta. With so many other royal Greek guests and their armed guards in and about the palace, Menelaus decided his most trustworthy warriors and Paris's guards should share the task, in the corridor outside the door to his chamber, of protecting the athlete prince of Troy who'd quickly become his friend.

Helen

Agamemnon and Clytemnestra shared the chamber next to mine, the one she'd occupied before their marriage. Soon after they arrived, they asked me to speak with them.

They sat on chairs next to one another in the front room of the chamber. I chose to sit on a chair facing them. Their servant brought us cups of wine.

Helen's Orphans

"We'd like to know," Clytemnestra said as soon as the servant left, "why Menelaus invited a Trojan prince to his birthday celebration and treats him as if he's his guest of honor."

I turned to Agamemnon. "I thought only you could be your brother's guest of honor."

Agamemnon glared at me. "We wish to speak plainly with you. We don't need to sit here and listen to your sassy remarks."

"Nor do I need to sit here," I said, "and listen to your bluster. You want a needless war with the Trojans. They pose no threat to you or any other Greek king. Menelaus and I don't want the war you want."

"Your words," Agamemnon said, "are very close to treason."

"Treason where?" I asked. "This is Sparta. You aren't the king of Sparta. You don't tell me what's treason in Sparta. As of tomorrow, when your brother turns eighteen, he, and only he, tells me what's treason in Sparta."

"What you say," Agamemnon said, "is treachery to all Greeks. You'd let those damned Trojans take our land away from us, drive us into the sea and put an end to Greece."

"Where's your proof," I asked , "they have either the desire or ability to do that?"

"You're a naive fool," Agamemnon said. "It's obvious they want what we have. It's obvious they want us gone. And it's obvious they've got Asian hordes behind them they can pay to do the fighting to achieve what they want."

The Asian hordes Agamemnon had referred to were the eastern allies Paris had mentioned, the allies he and other Trojans believed would let them face Greece alone in a war.

I looked at Agamemnon and shook my head. "You're a liar. You're inventing a crisis that doesn't exist. The Trojans admire their Greek neighbors. I have no doubt they'd like to be considered our equals. But you have no justification whatsoever for claiming they plan to annihilate us. What you want is a war you think you can easily win and become known to the multitudes as the greatest king Greece has ever seen. And you don't give a damn how many lives it takes, Greek or Trojan, to achieve your goal."

Ron Fritsch

Chapter Sixteen

Helen

During the festivities the evening before the day Menelaus turned eighteen, he and I introduced Paris to Achilles, Odysseus and the other Greek kings.

Paris told Achilles he'd wanted nothing more, from his early boyhood, than a chance to compete in the Greek games.

Achilles looked him up and down. "What games do you think you might beat me in?"

Paris laughed. "All of them."

As Menelaus busied himself being polite to the kings who'd become his equals the next day, I admit Paris and I danced together as if the royal wedding in Sparta to which these same kings had already been invited would be most unusual for two reasons. The bride would be a Greek orphan. The groom would be a Trojan prince.

Helen

When the time came the next morning for the guests to leave, Menelaus was in a meeting with Agamemnon and the former regents of Sparta. Menelaus would now have the Spartan treasury under his control. He could spend it to rebuild the Spartan army and help the Spartan people he believed his father Atreus and Agamemnon's regents had neglected.

As Paris and I prepared to step into the carriage that would take us to the harbor, he saw Clytemnestra approaching the carriage that would take her to Mycenae. Agamemnon would leave Sparta and go home later that day.

Paris knew the king of Mycenae was Menelaus's brother and the queen he'd recently married was my sister, but that was all he knew about Agamemnon and Clytemnestra. They'd both avoided having any contact with the Trojan prince Menelaus had foolishly invited to his birthday celebration.

Irrepressible eighteen-year-old youth that Paris was, though, he waved to Clytemnestra and laughed.

"I'm running off to Troy with your sister Helen," he shouted. "You'll receive an invitation to our wedding."

Timon

"Did you consider," I wondered aloud, looking at Helen, "Paris wasn't entirely joking? Did you think he would've run off with you if he'd gotten the chance to do it?"

Those were two more questions that didn't seem to bother Helen.

"If I hadn't already promised to marry Menelaus," Helen replied, "Paris might've asked me to marry him. I doubt I would've gone with him to Troy that morning, though. I'd only met him three days before. But I have to confess I would've given his proposal serious consideration. He was attractive, bright and kind. If he'd survived the war, I believe he would've been a good parent for any children he fathered."

Helen

Menelaus met me in the vegetable garden that afternoon. I was pulling weeds with the servants. Menelaus and I chose a place where we could pull weeds together and speak privately.

He told me his former regents hadn't shown up for their meeting with him that morning. During his birthday festivities, they and their families had left Sparta and gone to Mycenae. They'd secretly liquidated whatever assets, including their houses, they'd had in Sparta.

Agamemnon had arrived for the meeting alone. He told Menelaus the regents had fled, and he explained why they'd done it. He'd ordered them to take with them to Mycenae all but a small fraction of the silver and gold in the Spartan treasury.

"Your brother took it for himself?" I asked.

Menelaus nodded. "I knew his regents were dipping into the treasury all along. They were giving most of that to my brother too. They were only keeping a part of it for themselves."

"Did Agamemnon make any attempt to justify looting the Spartan treasury?"

"He said he took it to finance the coming war with Troy. He had no choice, he told me. He knew I'd never agree to use the Spartan silver and gold to fight a war with Troy. Under the circumstances, he said, I should be grateful he left me any at all."

"How much did he leave you?"

Menelaus gestured toward the servants working in the garden. "Enough to pay the people who work here and the few warriors the regents left me with."

Menelaus would have to wait for future tax receipts before he could embark upon any of the projects he'd hoped he could start when he became the ruling king. As for his plan to revive the Spartan army, that would also have to wait. Apart from his lack of silver and gold to pay for new warriors, the experienced warriors the regents had dismissed from the old Spartan army were now members of the Mycenean army and had sworn their loyalty to Agamemnon. They couldn't take back their oaths without facing executions for treason.

"He played me for a fool," Menelaus said. "He began planning this the day our father told the people he'd give each of us a kingdom. Agamemnon thought he, the older son, should inherit both kingdoms."

I shook my head. "But even without the treasury and the army, you're still the king of Sparta. You should tell the people what your brother has done."

Menelaus frowned. "I can't say anything about it publicly."

"Why can't you?"

"Agamemnon warned me he and the regents would deny they've done anything wrong. He'd declare war on me for slandering him, march his army into Sparta and depose me. Then he'd be what he was always supposed to be, the king of Mycenae *and* Sparta."

"And you'd be dead?"

"No doubt I would."

Like his two uncles his father Atreus had murdered, Menelaus hadn't imagined the extent of his brother's diabolical intentions.

Menelaus looked at me as if he were ready to weep. "Do you still want to marry me?"

I was surprised he'd asked me that question.

"I want to marry you more than ever," I said. "From this day forward, I'm going to spend every moment of my life helping you undo what your brother has done."

Timon

I could tell something bothered Lukas.

"We've heard," he said to Helen, "the festivities for your wedding to Menelaus were lavish. People came to the palace from all over Sparta to eat the king's food and drink his wine. With a nearly empty treasury, how did he pay for that?"

Helen shook her head. "He didn't pay for it. Agamemnon did."

"Agamemnon?" Lukas asked. "Why did he pay for your wedding? From what you've told us, it's difficult to believe he'd do anything at that point for you and Menelaus."

This time I was ahead of Lukas. I'd guessed what Helen would say.

"Agamemnon didn't do it as a favor to us," she replied. "Menelaus and I had decided we'd have a wedding with neither guests nor festivities. He was the ruling king. All he had to do was ask me if I wanted to marry him in front of witnesses, tell them he wanted to marry me, and declare us married. A few of his servants and warriors would've been perfectly adequate witnesses, and more than we needed legally. But when Agamemnon learned what we planned to do, he put a stop to it."

Lukas still hadn't gotten to the heart of the matter. "So why did Agamemnon do that? Why did he waste his stolen silver and gold on a wedding with the Greek kings and the Spartan people eating as much of his food and drinking as much of his wine as they pleased?"

Helen, who seemed to delight in innocence wherever she found it, looked at Lukas and smiled. "Agamemnon didn't want anybody to know he'd looted the Spartan treasury. He was afraid the wedding Menelaus and I decided to have would lead to questions he had no desire to hear or answer. The Spartan people were looking forward to our royal wedding. The last one they'd attended, when Atreus married the mother of Agamemnon and Menelaus, was many years in the past by then. If we deprived them of the usual royal wedding festivities, they'd surely suspect something was wrong. The other Greek kings would too."

"So Agamemnon," I said, "forced Menelaus to have a lavish wedding and not disappoint the Spartan people."

"That's what the bully Agamemnon did," Helen replied.

"And yet," I said, "Agamemnon could still claim he was far kinder to Menelaus than their father was to his brothers."

Helen scoffed. "Agamemnon was no kinder to Menelaus than their father was to the brothers he murdered. Agamemnon wanted to win

Achilles, Odysseus and Ajax over to his side in his argument for a war, led by him, against Troy. He knew he could never accomplish that if he killed another Greek king without having a damned good reason for doing it. No, he realized he was better off keeping his brother alive and paying for his lavish wedding, no matter how much it would cost him."

Helen took a drink of her water and gave me a wry smile.

"Clytemnestra," she said, "sent us a message saying she hoped we'd invited to our wedding the Trojan prince Menelaus and I liked so much. At the time, I assumed she was merely being her sarcastic self."

Helen

After Menelaus became the ruling king, persons with complaints filled his courtroom every morning. During the time the regents were in power, they'd taken bribes in almost every dispute they heard—as Clytemnestra would do in Mycenae during the Trojan War.

The regents had made it clear to all the litigants who offered them bribes, whether in winning or losing amounts, they'd severely punish anybody who complained about their corrupt style of governing. They guaranteed anybody who said anything about it to the naive boy king would be found dead.

Menelaus realized the regents had to flee to Sparta when he turned eighteen and they lost their authority to rule for him. They knew the boy king would place them on trial for treason.

In any event, many of the persons the regents had ruled against were asking Menelaus to reverse their rulings. They claimed the bribes paid to the regents had tainted their cases and therefore Menelaus should rehear them from their beginning. The former boy king agreed.

He and I ate our suppers together late every evening.

Helen

We had invited Paris to our wedding. Eager to return to Greece, he arrived several days before the other guests did. Menelaus once again shared his chamber with our Trojan friend.

But Menelaus was still spending long days in court and had little time to entertain Paris. I proposed taking our guest to as many of the towns and villages in Sparta as he and I could get to. I thought introducing the likable athlete prince to the people would help them see the Trojans weren't the fearsome, warlike savages Agamemnon had made them out to be. Menelaus agreed. He thought the tour I had in mind was a splendid idea.

Helen

So Paris and I, in a chariot pulled by Menelaus's horse, set out on our journey to meet the Spartan people. The three guards who came from Troy with Paris followed us in a carriage. Paris had asked them to keep their spears, swords and daggers hidden under blankets on the floor of the carriage. He didn't want Spartans to think he feared them.

Initially, the large crowds greeting us in every hamlet and town we came to surprised me. Then I realized the people had heard the foolish talk about the orphan girl who'd somehow become the most beautiful woman in the world. Within a few more days, she'd marry the boy king they'd also fallen in love with. She'd be their queen and make the fairy tale come true. That she'd arrive in their town or village accompanied not by the young king she'd marry but by an exotic foreign prince whose beauty was said to rival hers only intensified their desire to see their visitors.

Chapter Seventeen

Helen

W e arrived in a village whose inhabitants included a young woman considered the best archer in Greece. She'd heard Paris had bragged to Achilles one of the sports he excelled in was archery.

What could Paris do but agree to a contest with her before we left for the next town? Since he hadn't brought his bow and arrows with him, she told him he could use hers.

"That's an advantage to your Trojan friend right there," her grandmother told me. "She makes her own bows and arrows. I taught her how to do it. They're the finest in Greece."

As the game proceeded in the usual fashion, with increasing target distances for each round, one of the Trojan guards told a large number of the villagers a story concerning Paris.

"He was only fourteen years old at the time," the guard said.

The prince had gone out to the countryside to participate in, and win, an archery competition. As he walked back to Troy, he saw a farmer's son running toward him. While the boy's family was attending the archery competition that afternoon, three thieves had made off with their cattle. They weren't far away yet, though. Could Paris attempt to stop them using his bow and arrows?

Paris and the boy ran in the direction the thieves had gone. They caught up with the boy's father, who was still some distance from the thieves and the cattle herd. The farmer asked Paris if he could shoot the thieves from there. Paris said he'd try to do it, but if he missed the thieves, he might hit some of the cattle. The farmer told him he'd take his chances. He wanted the thieves stopped as soon as possible.

The first arrow Paris shot sliced into the lower back of the nearest thief, who screamed, causing his fellow rustlers to turn on their heels and expose their bellies to Paris, whose next two arrows, quickly handed to him by the farmer and his son, sank deep into their guts.

The cries of the wounded rustlers sent the cattle running. Paris handed his bow to the farmer's son and began running himself, toward the cattle.

As the farmer's family watched, stunned, Paris loped across the plain, caught up with and then ran ahead of the cattle. He turned around and, running backwards now as if he did it every day, faced the herd. He waved his arms above his head and slowed the animals to a halt.

"Go home now," he instructed the cattle, in a soothing voice, as if he were a parent and they were his children. "Go home now."

The cattle turned and began their walk homeward. When they passed the moaning thieves, each of them lying on the ground with an arrow protruding from his body, they lowered their heads and stared at them. Perhaps they hadn't previously seen humans so reduced in power and possibility.

Paris herded the cattle back to their pasture and closed the gate behind them. The farmer and his family walked toward the fourteen-year-old prince speechless.

The two cattle thieves Paris shot in their bellies died of their wounds that same day. As soon as Priam and Hecuba discovered what had happened, they ordered the third thief taken from his deathbed and hanged.

"Is that story true?" one of the Spartan villagers asked. "Or is it a tale the Trojan people like to tell about a prince they favor?"

"It's true," the guard who'd told the story said.

"How do you know it's true?" the villager asked.

The guard looked at me and grinned. I'd heard him tell the story before.

The guard turned to the villager. "I was there. I saw what happened. I was the farmer's son who asked Paris if he could stop the thieves. I was fourteen, the same age as Paris."

I'd enjoyed hearing the guard's story a second time, but he'd left one thing out.

"Why don't you explain," I asked him, "why you left your family's farm and why you're here in Greece with Paris?"

"The prince stayed overnight with my family," the guard replied. "The next day I walked to Troy with him. I'd offered to protect him to the end of my life or his. My family had encouraged me to do it. I had two sisters and two brothers who could stay on the farm and take care of our parents in their old age. I enjoyed learning about the world with Paris during his lessons with his tutors. We heard how inventive and admirable the Greeks were—how ruthless they could be too."

Helen's Orphans

Helen

There was almost no breeze that warm and humid afternoon. Paris and his Greek opponent shot nothing but bull's eyes from every distance.

"It's a tie," the Greek archer said.

"It's a tie," Paris agreed, "but it's also a victory for me."

"How is it a victory for you?" his opponent asked.

Paris laughed. "I tied the best archer in Greece. Nobody in Troy can remember a Trojan doing that. Wouldn't you call that a victory?"

"It might be more of a victory for all of us," the Greek archer said, "if being a Greek or a Trojan didn't matter."

"If we were just competitors in a sport?" Paris asked.

The Greek archer nodded. "Just competitors in a sport."

Helen

After the archery contest, athletes challenged Paris to compete with them in every town we came to. The people we met also wanted to hear the story about Paris and the cattle thieves.

The farmers' son and the other guards were like the boyhood friends they'd been, loudly cheering Paris on. As the bride-to-be of Menelaus, I couldn't take sides against a fellow Spartan, of course, but I could congratulate our Trojan guest whenever he won and thank whoever had competed against him.

Timon

"Did you ever fear," Lukas asked Helen, "your tour of Sparta with Paris would come back to haunt you—people would condemn you for flaunting a new lover?"

Helen shook her head. "I never imagined anybody would question what Paris and I did. He and I never shared a moment alone together. We never slept overnight in the same house. He had his three guards with him at all times. Paris's father and mother and brother had ordered them to stay close to him. Their failure to do that would've been treason. No, I never dreamed anybody would claim Paris and I had done anything wrong. Everybody we met seemed to understand we were

129

touring Sparta to convince the people the war Agamemnon wanted to fight against Troy would be unnecessary, pointless and wrong."

Helen

But the kindly sentiments towards Trojans that Paris and I encountered during our tour of Sparta would soon evaporate like morning dew under a hot summer sun.

The archer Paris fought to a tie was the one who took a shot at me when she saw me looking down from a watchtower early in the war in Troy. She was also the archer who, in the last days of the war, fatally wounded Paris a moment after his arrow had pierced Achilles's heart.

I never blamed her for shooting either of those arrows. She'd only done what a warrior was supposed to do. Her arrows were meant to kill us. That's what war was. And that's why I came to believe leaders who care for their people only fight a war if they have no other choice.

Helen

The day before the day I was to marry Menelaus, Paris and his guards and I joined the Spartans converging on the palace for the nuptial festivities.

That afternoon I stood with Menelaus on the balcony outside his chamber, waving to the wedding guests who assumed they were feasting on the king's ample supplies of food, drinking as much from his vessels of wine as they wished, and dancing to the tunes of the musicians he'd paid.

Even as the crowd cheered, though, I noticed an apprehensive look on Menelaus's face.

"I don't like what I see out there," he said.

"What don't you like? The people love you."

"I don't doubt that. But my brother's warriors—posing as civilians—are among them."

"More than a few of them?"

"Many more than a few of them. His entire army must be in Sparta. And all of them are posing as civilians. They're cheering too."

Helen

Helen's Orphans

After Menelaus and I reentered his chamber from the balcony, we found Agamemnon and Clytemnestra standing in the front room as if they'd been waiting for us. Ordinarily, when guests came to see the ruling king, one of the warriors performing guard duty would knock on the door to the chamber, come in when bidden, and disclose who wished see him.

"Have my warriors fallen asleep?" Menelaus asked.

"My warriors are outside your door now," Agamemnon replied.

"Where are mine?" Menelaus asked.

"My warriors have removed them from the palace. They're on the road to Mycenae. I promise I'll take good care of them as long as you and Helen cooperate with what we've got planned for you."

"Cooperate?" I asked Agamemnon. "What have you got planned for us?"

Clytemnestra laughed. "You'll run off to Troy with your lover Paris," she said. "You'll do it in the morning."

"I'll never do that," I said.

Agamemnon snickered. "You'll do it."

"Paris isn't my lover," I said. "I have no desire to run off with him to Troy. The person I love stands next to me. I intend to marry him tomorrow. I also intend to share his bed with him tomorrow night. Paris will go home to Troy with his guards."

Agamemnon shook his head. "If you wish to remain alive, you'll run off to Troy tomorrow with that pretty-boy prince. We'll tell the people he abducted you."

"Paris would never abduct me," I said.

Agamemnon looked at me as if he and I were conspirators. "We'll *tell the people* the Trojan prince and his guards abducted you. You don't want the Greek people believing you ran off with him of your own free will. In any event, you and he will leave on his ship sailing to Troy tomorrow. Otherwise, you and a number of other people will be dead before tomorrow is over. I have more than enough warriors in and around this palace to make that happen. They came with the crowds from the towns and villages of Sparta on their merry way to the palace for what they thought would be wedding festivities."

Clytemnestra laughed again. "Those Spartans will learn tomorrow they've been celebrating a wedding that had to be canceled when the bride failed to show up for it."

131

Menelaus turned to Agamemnon. "You're doing this to start a war with Troy."

Agamemnon laughed. "You're damned right that's what I'm doing."

Menelaus shook his head. "You haven't been able to convince Achilles, Odysseus and Ajax a war with Troy is necessary. They don't think a few pirates are worth fighting a war over."

"They don't think the eventual extermination of the Greeks at the hands of the blood-thirsty, upstart Trojans is worth fighting a war over. They can't peer into the future as well as I can. But I can see our best opportunity to stop those Trojans is now."

Menelaus scowled. "And you think you can change the minds of the Greek kings if a Trojan prince steals Helen away from me the morning of my wedding day."

Agamemnon laughed. "That's what this is all about."

"You hope," Menelaus said, "if a Trojan prince runs off with a Greek king's bride-to-be, Achilles, Odysseus and Ajax will view the Trojans as you do—as increasingly powerful and evil neighbors across the sea who wish to see us dead and take our lands."

I turned to Agamemnon. "Who, besides myself, will you kill tomorrow if I don't set foot on that ship bound for Troy?"

"Menelaus is the second person on my list," Agamemnon replied.

"You'd kill your own brother?"

"He's a traitor to Greece, the same as you. He let you tour Sparta with an enemy prince. I have others on my list as well."

"Who are the others?" I asked.

"Menelaus's warriors—they'll die for sure. They chose to stay here with him to the end. They didn't want to fight for me. I'll gladly let them know what that'll cost them."

"Who else will you kill?" Menelaus asked.

Agamemnon turned to his brother. "Your servants. They always loved the good prince, you, and hated the bad prince, me. Now they'll hate the bad prince even more."

"What about their children?" I asked.

Agamemnon laughed. "I'll send them to the orphanage you came from."

Clytemnestra turned to me. "I placed another person on my husband's list—someone you especially don't want to see on it."

"Who's that?" I asked.

Helen's Orphans

Clytemnestra looked at me the way she did whenever she knew she'd done something clever to vex me.

"Leda," she replied. "We know she's here for what was supposed to be your wedding."

It took me more than a few moments to comprehend what Clytemnestra had told me.

"Leda was like a mother to us," I said. "Why would you place her on a list of people to be killed for what I refuse to do?"

Clytemnestra scoffed. "She wasn't much of a mother to me. You were always her favorite. But think about it. She'll die if you don't do what the greatest king in Greece asks you to do tomorrow. Would you like to see your precious Leda with her throat slit open moments before you taste the sword yourself?"

Ron Fritsch

Chapter Eighteen

Helen

Menelaus turned to Agamemnon. "What if Paris doesn't wish to run off with Helen? What if he's too decent to do that? What if he'd rather not steal another person's bride-to-be—even if he has fallen in love with her himself?"

Agamemnon seemed unconcerned, as if his brother's words were as soundless as leaves falling in autumn.

"Paris is an honorable person," I chose to add. "He'll never do what you want him to do."

Agamemnon looked at me and shrugged. "If the Trojan prince doesn't do what I want him to do, please let him know he'll die. So will his guards. It's as simple as that."

"You'll kill perfectly innocent people," I said, "to start a ludicrous, hateful war."

Agamemnon turned to Menelaus. "When you looked down on the deliriously happy, drunken crowd from your balcony, did you see how close several of my warriors were to the Trojan prince and his guards? Did you see they could've reached out with their daggers on a signal and killed them all?"

Menelaus took a deep breath. "I saw them. I saw what they could do."

"Good," Agamemnon said. "My warriors will remain close enough to kill them up to the moment they embark on the ship returning them to Troy. Helen will be with them, or they'll never set foot on that ship again. They'll be dead. So will she and you and all those others."

Menelaus took another deep breath. "How could you ever justify so much killing?"

Agamemnon smirked. "I happened upon a conspiracy to commit treason against all the Greek kingdoms. The foolish young king of Sparta and his scheming bride-to-be were conspiring with a Trojan prince to hand Greece over to our enemy. I had no time to waste. I had to kill them all or suffer the dreadful consequences of doing nothing to stop the traitors."

"And killing the Trojan prince and his guards," Menelaus said, "would also get you a war with Troy. Achilles, Odysseus and Ajax would have no say in the matter. The father, mother and brother of the dead Trojan prince would be bound to go to war with Greece whether they wanted one or not. No matter what Helen, Paris and I decide to do, you'll have the war you seek."

Clytemnestra looked at me and laughed. "I ended up the queen of a great king of Greece. You chose to marry a king who has no treasury and no army. Can you admit now, at last, you've lost and I've won?"

I couldn't imagine how a war with Troy would make either of us a winner.

"I've lost," I asked, "because I chose to marry a decent, kind and gentle human? You've won because you settled for a demon like his father who'd murder anybody, including his brother, to get what he wants?"

Clytemnestra laughed. "You chose to marry a fool like yourself. I settled on a king who knows what it takes to rule his people."

Agamemnon looked at me again as if I should've been happy to play my part in his scheme.

"To tell you the truth," he said, "I hope I don't have to kill you or anybody else on my list. You can go off with that prince everybody says you've fallen in love with. You can do it with a clear conscience. You can always tell yourself I gave you no other choice. I even hope you marry your prince and enjoy your lust together as much and as long as you can. My poor brother here will never be able to claim he spent so much as one night in bed with you. But he's always been a loser. No, I hope you choose to live. I don't really want to kill any Greeks, not even those warriors who spurned me or those servants who detested me. I want to kill Trojans. I want to see all of them dead and their city in flames."

Helen

Agamemnon told one of his warriors dressed as a civilian to pretend he was a messenger from Menelaus, find Paris in the crowd, and ask him to come to the king's chamber. Menelaus and I were to speak with him alone.

Helen's Orphans

"He's on my list," Agamemnon reminded us. "If he doesn't want to die, if he doesn't want to see his guards dead, he'll know what to do."

Helen

Paris sat on a chair opposite ours in the front room as Menelaus and I explained the ultimatum Agamemnon had given us.

When we were done, Paris looked at Menelaus and shook his head. "I'll never ask Helen to run off with me. That's the most disgusting thing I've ever heard of. I'll never do it. I can see how much you love her."

He looked at me as if he'd been given a death sentence and had only moments to live.

"Don't get me wrong," he said. "If you'd never promised to marry Menelaus tomorrow, I'd run off with you to wherever in this world you chose to go. I'd become a shepherd in a distant land, with people speaking a language I'd never heard before, if you wanted me to."

"We know that," Menelaus said. "We know you're in love with Helen. We also know you'd never attempt to steal her away from me."

"We all know that," I said.

Paris turned to Menelaus again. "So what do we do? I've heard Achilles and Odysseus are here. Can't we tell them what your brother is doing? Won't they stop him?"

Menelaus shook his head. "We can't do that."

"Achilles and Odysseus are here as wedding guests," I said. "Unfortunately, they left their armies home in Phthia and Ithaca. On the other hand, Agamemnon's entire army is here, in Sparta, and we have no army."

Menelaus nodded. "Agamemnon warned us we have to keep our mouths shut. Only he and Clytemnestra and the three of us are to know what he's doing. The moment any other people find out about this, he'll assume one of us told them. We'll die, and the others he threatened to kill will die with us. Your guards. My warriors and servants. Even the woman who was like a mother to Helen in the orphanage. I don't want to see either you or Helen or any of those other people killed, but I have no doubt Agamemnon would do it. He admired our father for killing his brothers, who were losers and fools like me."

Paris looked at me as if Achilles had him on his back in a wrestling match.

"So what do we do?" he asked again.

"Menelaus and I have made a decision," I replied, "if you agree to it. In the morning I'll be on your ship with you. I'll go with you to Troy."

Paris opened his eyes wide. "You'll go with me to Troy?"

"Agamemnon told us," I said, "we'll have to maintain our silence even after we're in Troy. If we don't, and word of his role in our elopement or abduction, or whatever he wants to call it, gets back to Greece, he'll kill Menelaus and all those other Spartans on his list."

Paris closed his eyes and shook his head. "I never would've come to Greece if I'd thought this would happen."

"We know that," Menelaus said. "Just help us get around a lot of unnecessary bloodshed."

Helen

Paris agreed to comply with Agamemnon's demands. Before he left Menelaus and me, he told us he'd inform his guards I'd agreed to run off to Troy with him in the morning. He doubted, though, as I did, they'd send up a cheer when they heard the news.

Helen

After Menelaus and I were alone again, he looked at me. "I can't imagine Achilles, Odysseus and Ajax will agree to a war merely because a Trojan prince has run off with my bride-to-be. They'll laugh and be glad it didn't happen to them. If there's no war, I'm sure you'll be able to find a Greek ship to come home on."

"Maybe I can imagine what you can't," I said. "The kings of Greece are here for the wedding of one of their own. If a Trojan prince steals the bride and reduces the event to a joke, kings as filled with themselves as Achilles, Odysseus and Ajax might consider the theft a personal affront, especially if they believe the Trojan has forced the bride to go with him. Should a great people like the Greeks suffer humiliation like that without some kind of retaliation?"

Menelaus shook his head. "Some kind of retaliation doesn't have to include a war. We could secretly order our merchant ships to stay away from Troy. Then we could seize the Trojan merchant ships in our harbors. We could agree to let them go as soon as you returned home."

Helen's Orphans

I stared at Menelaus and knew how much I'd miss him. He was the youngest king in Greece and yet, as far as I could see, the most reasonable.

"If there is a war," Menelaus said, "and you can't come home, you should consider marrying Paris."

I at first had as much difficulty comprehending that advice as I'd had Clytemnestra's revelation that she'd added Leda to Agamemnon's death list.

"But I want to marry you," I said. "I want to share a bed with you."

"And I want you to marry me and share a bed with me. More than anything else, that's what I want. But look at the monsters we have for a brother and a sister and what they've contrived for us. We live in a world we had no hand in creating, but we still have to do the best we can in it. If you get stuck in Troy, don't reject Paris because you promised to marry me. I love you, Helen, and I want you to be as happy as you can be in this evil world."

Helen

Shortly before dawn on what was supposed to be my wedding day, Paris and I left the rear entrance of the palace together, running towards the woods at the end of the lawn.

Agamemnon had carefully stationed his warriors so that none of them would see me voluntarily leaving the palace with the Trojan prince.

Three young men reclining on the palace lawn, though, surely did see us. They appeared to be shepherds, unless they were wearing sheepskins as costumes to amuse themselves during the wedding festivities. When Paris and I reached the woods at the end of the lawn, one of them, who maybe hadn't drunk as much free wine as his comrades had, got to his feet and followed us, at a distance, through the woods.

He was still tracking us when we reached the guards and the carriage they'd brought to Sparta. I'm certain he could see I got into the carriage without being forced to do it.

I began to wonder if what the shepherd and his two friends had witnessed would force Agamemnon to admit I'd run off with Paris voluntarily. I couldn't hope, though, that would stop Agamemnon from demanding the Greeks go to war with the Trojans if they refused to return me to Sparta and the king I was supposed to marry there.

Timon

Lukas chose not to tell Helen his uncle was the shepherd who'd spied on her and Paris as they hurried from the palace and through the woods on the morning of her wedding day.

He had something else to say to Helen. "You were in love with both Menelaus and Paris."

Helen looked at Lukas as if she'd also fallen in love with him.

"I was," she replied. "That was my secret. I was in love with Menelaus as well as Paris. If I could've married both of them that day, and if they'd agreed to my sharing beds with them on alternate nights, I would've done it."

Lukas turned to me. "If I fell in love with another person, would you agree to my sharing beds with you and him on alternate nights?"

I thought about the question a few moments before I answered it.

Then I shrugged. "If you found somebody else you truly felt was as good for you as I am, I'd have no objection."

Chapter Nineteen

Timon

Prior to our conversation with Helen in the royal olive grove, neither Lukas nor I had heard anything leading us to suspect Agamemnon had forced Helen and Paris to leave Sparta and go to Troy together.

I turned to Helen. "Do other people know the story you've told us?"

"Very few," she replied. "Until today, Menelaus and I and three others have been the only living persons who've known what I told you. The additional people who ever knew it—Paris, Agamemnon and Clytemnestra—are dead."

"Who are the three other living persons who know the story?" I asked.

"Hermione and Orestes are two of them," Helen replied. "Menelaus and I told them when we became certain we could trust them not to speak of the matter with other people."

"Orestes," I asked, "knew the story when he sentenced his mother to death?"

Helen nodded. "He did."

"You and Menelaus," I asked, "have been like a mother and father to him?"

Helen appeared to like my question. "From the day we brought him here to live with us."

"The people seem to think," I said, "when he sentenced his mother to die, he was seeking revenge for the murder of his father. But was he?"

Helen shrugged. "You'd have to ask him about that, but I think it's unlikely he was."

Timon

"Who's the fifth living person who knew the story before today?" I asked.

That seemed to be another question Helen wanted to answer. "Leda. She takes a special interest, you know, in our swans. Their pond isn't far from here. I'll have to show it to you. It's a beautiful place. She keeps it that way herself."

"Why does she know the story you've told us?" Lukas asked.

Helen hesitated before she gave us an answer to that question, but then she came out with it. "Leda isn't just the only person in my life who's been like a parent to me. She's in fact my mother."

Lukas and I took a few moments to consider those remarks.

Lukas broke the silence. "Was Leda also Clytemnestra's mother?"

"She was," Helen replied. "Clytemnestra and I were the only children she had. Hermione and Orestes are her grandchildren. She's very close to both of them."

Helen fought back tears before she continued her story.

"Menelaus," she said, "kept Leda informed from the day I went to Troy. He felt she needed to know the peril Clytemnestra and Agamemnon had placed her in."

"Was Leda the person," Lukas asked, "who left you and Clytemnestra in a basket outside the main gate to the orphanage?"

"She was," Helen replied. "She hid behind the shrubbery there and kept an eye on us until the guardians found us. Then she applied for a position at the orphanage so she could continue to watch over us. Few people wanted to work at the orphanage in those days. She turned out to be an excellent orphanage guardian even at a time when she didn't need to be. She never found it necessary to lay a hand on a child."

Lukas seemed as puzzled as I was. "Why did Leda put her daughters in an orphanage?"

"She had no other choice," Helen replied. "If she hadn't done that, my father's family—he was Clytemnestra's father too—would've had all three of us killed."

"Who was your father?" I asked.

Helen hesitated again but knew she had to tell us who he was.

"Ajax," she said.

Timon

Helen told us Leda's story. She was the daughter of servants who worked in the palace in Salamis. The young children of servants who couldn't fend for themselves were locked together in a poorly attended basement room while their parents worked.

Helen's Orphans

Early on, Leda found the palace library a refuge and spent her days in it teaching herself to read and write. After she'd accomplished that, every document in the library became accessible to her, and she went on to learn as many other things as she wished.

When the time came for the prince, Ajax, to learn to read and write and do arithmetic, his father and mother, the king and queen of Salamis, realized they had a daughter of servants who could earn her keep by teaching their son everything the prince would need to know. Leda, who was the same age as Ajax, readily agreed to be his tutor.

Leda the servants' daughter and Ajax the prince grew up together, first as teacher and pupil but later as lovers. Leda told Helen she'd read stories giving her ample warning not to do what she did. She nevertheless chose to believe Ajax when he told her his father and mother would be pleased to consent to his marriage to a child of servants who'd proven herself to be, as he described her, the most excellent instructor for a royal heir in all of Greece.

After Leda became pregnant with Clytemnestra, Ajax declined to seek his parents' consent to his marriage to Leda. He refused to do it, he said, not because she was a daughter of servants but because the time for his marriage hadn't arrived yet. And even though Ajax and Leda were both eighteen years old then, she chose to believe him once more.

She found an abandoned house in the royal forest, made it livable for herself and went missing from the palace. Her absence, though, provoked little comment and even less concern. She was an only child whose parents had gone to the bottom of the sea in a sailboat. Ajax's drunken older sister, whose love for her maid hadn't been requited, was at the helm when the boat went down. She and the maid also perished in the disaster.

Ajax came to see Leda almost daily. He brought with him on his chariot whatever she needed but couldn't find in the forest. Her prince, she enjoyed telling him, had become her servant. His loads weren't burdensome, though. The kindling in the forest provided her an endless supply of fuel for her fireplace. She taught herself how to take down a deer with a bow and arrow, butcher it and preserve its meat. She learned which plants and mushrooms she should leave where they grew and which she'd enjoy, cooked or raw, on her plate.

Leda went through two pregnancies and gave birth twice as the other forest denizens did—unassisted. But Ajax still hadn't asked his father and mother for their consent to his marriage to the mother of his daughters. At that point Leda told him he'd either seek their approval or no longer share her bed.

Ajax chose to face his parents. He returned to the forest from the palace, though, with the worst possible news. The king and queen had told him they'd never consent to the marriage of their son to a child of servants. They also gave Ajax two choices. He and Leda could secretly place their two daughters in an orphanage in another kingdom—the one in Sparta would do—and have no further contact with them or each other. They'd also never reveal the existence of the daughters. Otherwise, the king and queen would have Leda and her daughters killed.

Timon

"I assume Leda did the sewing," I said.

Helen nodded. "She sewed Clytemnestra's name and birth date with blue thread because she'd run out of the green thread she favored sewing mine."

"But Leda," I said, "didn't comply with the part of the order requiring she have nothing further to do with her daughters."

Helen's face brightened as if she'd emerged from the darkness of a forest and stepped into sunlight on a meadow. "Nobody in Sparta knew who Leda was. She'd changed her name. She hadn't been known as Leda in Salamis."

"When did you learn," I asked, "Leda and Ajax were your mother and father?"

"When I reached my fifteenth birthday," Helen replied, "Leda told me her story."

"Did she tell Clytemnestra her story?" I asked.

Helen shook her head. "She never trusted Clytemnestra would keep the story a secret. Leda and I agreed on that. Clytemnestra would always be too tempted to prove her claim to be a royal daughter. That sort of thing was important to her."

"Did Ajax know," I asked, "he was your and Clytemnestra's father?"

Helen looked at me as if I'd suddenly become a thumb-sucking boy again.

Helen's Orphans

"Of course he did," she said. "He knew our names. He knew how old we were. He and everybody else knew the sisters Agamemnon and Menelaus chose to marry had grown up in the orphanage in Sparta. At Agamemnon's wedding and Menelaus's birthday celebration, Ajax couldn't take his eyes off Clytemnestra and me. She thought he was a horny old king trying to flirt with two much younger women. I knew he was staring at his daughters, probably recalling his days and nights in the forest with Leda. But he didn't dare tell anybody he was our father. His mother was still alive. She could've sent assassins to kill us."

Lukas had another question concerning Ajax. "Why did he throw himself on his sword after the war?"

Helen shrugged. "My guess is, he was ashamed of what he'd done."

"What he'd done to Leda and his daughters?" I asked.

Helen shrugged again. "That might've been part of what bothered him. I think, though, he must've been more ashamed of giving in to Agamemnon and agreeing to participate in a futile, costly, tragic war. He didn't want to come home to Greece and face his people. Maybe, because he was my father, and my mother had loved him in his youth, I'm hoping that's why he did himself in. Other people say he took his life because he hadn't gained nearly as much glory in the war as the younger Achilles and Odysseus had. I've always thought that was a ridiculous explanation. The war was stupid, like most wars. Achilles and Odysseus only proved what fools they were for playing their parts in it. I can't imagine future generations will look back on anybody gaining any glory in the Trojan War. I'm certain the excuse for it alone—my elopement or abduction—will always make it seem absurd, to say the least."

Timon

Lukas wasn't done with his interrogation of Helen. "Why have only five people known the truth? Why don't all the people know the stories they tell about you aren't true? Both of them are false. You never chose to run off to Troy, and Paris never abducted you. Why haven't you told the people Agamemnon forced you and Paris and Menelaus to do what you did?"

Helen nodded as if to indicate she'd known she'd need to answer those questions.

145

"When I came back to Greece," she said, "Menelaus and I agreed to keep the true story a secret. We clearly had no choice as long as Agamemnon was still alive. But even after his death, we knew we couldn't tell the people the truth."

"I don't understand," I said. "You and Menelaus were perfectly innocent. Why wouldn't you want the people to know that?"

Helen shook her head. "We appear to have been perfectly innocent to you and Lukas today, seventeen years after the war ended. Back then, though, we couldn't imagine the people of Sparta and Greece would've agreed we were innocent."

"I still don't understand," I said.

"You don't understand," Helen said, "because you don't know how much the Greek people had suffered during the war—and continued to suffer for a number of years after it was over. And their suffering came about only because Menelaus and I had chosen to save our lives and the lives of about forty other Greeks and four Trojans. But many, many more Greeks and Trojans than that died because we'd given in to Agamemnon without making the slightest attempt to oppose him. If Menelaus and I had told the people the truth after Agamemnon died, we were certain they would've risen up against us, called us Agamemnon's collaborators and had us executed for treason. They would've said we did what we did only to save our own lives and the lives of people close to us. They would've argued we didn't do what we did for the good of Sparta or Greece but only for our spineless selves. I would've been tempted to agree with them."

Helen's comments left Lukas and me, for the time being at least, with nothing to say.

"After Agamemnon died," Helen said, "and his military commanders gave Menelaus and me a second kingdom to rule, we decided we wanted to stay alive and rule both of them for the benefit of the people and not for a royal family and its favorites. To do that, though, we'd have to appear to have been what Agamemnon had said we were—the victims of the extraordinary lust of an evil Trojan prince. We were fortunate that shepherd who saw Paris and me running across the lawn and through the woods never came forward."

"Maybe," Lukas said, "he feared contradicting Agamemnon."

Helen's Orphans

Helen nodded. "I've always assumed that was the case. I've often wondered what happened to him. He must've been taken to Troy with the other shepherds his age."

I waited for Lukas to respond to that, but he chose not to.

I turned to Helen. "If the Greek people had risen up against you and Menelaus after you told them the truth, they would've sailed home from one tragedy only to embark upon another."

"That might be true," she said, "but I very much doubt the Greek people who survived the war would've seen things that way. The question for Menelaus and me is whether we could change our story now and tell the people the truth."

"I think you could," I said. "You and Menelaus and Paris made a choice to save the lives of more than forty human beings. You had no way to know for certain what the consequences of making that choice would be. The three of you doubted Achilles, Odysseus, Ajax and the other Greek kings would start a horrible war just to bring you back to Greece. The Greek kings could've done what you and Menelaus wanted them to do. They could've seized some Trojan merchant ships and held them hostage until the Trojans sent you home. They didn't need to attempt to kill every living Trojan and reduce their city to rubble."

"I agree," Lukas said, turning to Helen. "The lives of those forty people were in certain and immediate jeopardy. You and Menelaus believed Agamemnon's warriors could've and would've killed you and the others if you'd dared to oppose him. The consequences of your choice not to oppose him might've been nothing more serious, for all you knew, than the amusement people enjoy at the expense of a cuckolded king."

Helen laughed. "Menelaus and I believe the Greek people can now look back at our choice not to oppose Agamemnon as reasonably as you and Timon do. But I'm certain very few Greeks, for many years after the war, would've been so dispassionate about it. They would've had people to blame, and punish, for what they'd gone through—Menelaus and me."

Ron Fritsch

Chapter Twenty

Timon

Menelaus and I had another reason," Helen said, "for not telling the people the truth about what happened before I sailed to Troy with Paris. My story wouldn't be complete if I didn't tell you what that reason was. You wouldn't fully know why we've chosen secrecy over the truth during the seventeen years since the end of the war."

"I want to hear the whole story," I said.

"So do I," Lukas said.

Looking at me, Helen nodded. "Then here it is. Paris and I had a child in Troy. The child was legitimate. We were married ten months when he was born. Paris was clearly the boy's father. He was the only person I'd been intimate with."

Lukas and I looked at one another before we turned to Helen again.

Lukas, though, asked the question before I could get it out of my mouth. "What happened to the boy?"

"After the war," Helen said, "Menelaus and I brought him back to Sparta with us. He was a year old by then. But we knew we had to conceal his identity. To the people, he would've been the son of an abductor, a rapist, who was also an evil Trojan prince. They never would've let that person's son live in Greece. They would've torn him from my arms and killed him."

"What happened to the boy" Lukas asked again.

"The orphan children of Spartan warriors and workers who'd been killed in Troy were in the hold of the merchant ship we sailed home on. Menelaus placed the boy I'd given birth to with them. The people who'd taken care of the orphans in Troy accompanied them. You came home to Sparta in the hold of that ship, Lukas. I remember being told who your parents were, where they'd come from and how they'd been killed."

"But nobody knew who your child's parents were?" I asked, my voice breaking.

Helen shook her head. "Menelaus told the caregivers he'd found the boy among the corpses of a group of Greek warriors and workers who'd been killed in the closing days of the war. He said the Trojans had apparently spared the child because he was so young. But nobody could remember whose child he was. Menelaus suggested a name and a birth date they could use for the boy. He knew, of course, those were the boy's actual name and birth date. He'd gotten them from me. Because he was the king, the caregivers used the name and birth date he'd suggested they use. They sewed them in the boy's tunic."

Knowing the truth now, I looked at Helen and struggled to hold back my tears.

"After Agamemnon died," Lukas said, "you and Menelaus could've told the people the boy's father wasn't a rapist but a man you loved and married. Why didn't you do that?"

"No," I said, without taking my eyes off Helen, "they couldn't do that. They would've had to tell the people the whole story about Agamemnon forcing them and Paris to do what they did."

Helen nodded. "That's right. But even if we'd convinced the people the boy's father wasn't a Trojan rapist, he was still Paris. He was the sharpshooting archer who'd killed and injured far more Greeks than any other Trojan had. His victims included workers as well as warriors. And the last arrow he shot pierced the heart of the great Achilles himself. No son of that Trojan prince would've survived in Greece in the first years after the war. Whether Menelaus and I wanted to keep the child alive or not, other Spartans and Greeks would've killed him as soon as they discovered who he was. They never would've listened to any argument by us that Paris did nothing wrong and was only attempting to stop an unjustified invasion of his people's city. Menelaus and I could see we had no choice. If we wanted to keep the son of Paris and myself alive— and we very much did—we had to do everything we could to conceal his identity. Many Greeks wanted me tried for treason and executed for helping Paris kill such a large number of people in the war. Everybody knew I'd held his shield for him. Menelaus married me the day we returned to Sparta to put an end to the talk of my being tried for treason. But the son of Paris? What defense would he have had?"

"What happened to the boy?" Lukas asked a third time.

Helen looked at Lukas as if she were about to divulge a secret to a lover.

Helen's Orphans

"My son and you," she said, "and all the other orphans on the ship that brought us home were taken to the orphanage in Sparta. He grew up there."

I could no longer hold back my tears. The war had ended seventeen years ago, when I was one year old. And I was the only child in the orphanage whose mother and father had never been identified. Now I knew why.

"Which of the boys at the orphanage was he?" Lukas asked, the tremble in his voice revealing he knew by then as well as I did who the boy was.

Helen, herself in tears, turned to me. "The boy was you, Timon. You're my son. You were born in Troy. Paris was your father."

She and I rose from our chairs. She embraced me.

I welcomed her embrace.

She beckoned Lukas to join us.

He rose from his chair and wrapped his arms around us both.

I'd discovered the answer to my question, the one I'd asked at the end of my song.

Who was I?

Timon

"The true story," Helen said, after we'd wiped away our tears and resumed sitting in our chairs, "always included you, Timon. Menelaus and I couldn't tell the people that story without endangering you. When you were younger, we couldn't even tell you the story. You might've mistakenly thought you could tell others who you were. You might've jeopardized yourself. We couldn't let you do that."

"I understand," I said. "I'm grateful you and Menelaus kept me alive."

"It was the only thing we could do," Helen said. "I was your mother, and Menelaus and I both loved your father."

Lukas and I looked at one another again. We understood.

"But now," Helen said, "you're both on the eve of becoming adults. Menelaus and I agreed long ago the decision whether to tell the people our true story would be yours, Timon, when you came of age. We doubt, as you do, the truth would threaten any of us now. Like yourselves, more than half of the Greek people are too young to have any personal memory of the Trojan War. And for the people who suffered during the war and after it, I think they'll now be able to place the blame for the war not on your father Paris, Menelaus or me but where it belongs—on Agamemnon and Clytemnestra. And no more harm can come to them now."

"I think," I said, "we should tell the people the true story. I think the time has come for them to hear it."

"I agree," Lukas said. "People like my uncle—people who suffered during and after the war, and still do—need to hear the true story. Then they'll know in full, without a detail left out, the tragedy they survived. They'll see how easily humans lusting for power and glory can use the hatred of one people for another to obtain what they delude themselves they need. The true story will be a lesson for the ages. Maybe a war like the one that gave birth to orphans like me will never happen again."

And Lukas claimed I was a dreamer.

Timon

"You have another choice to make," Helen said. "Both of you have a choice to make."

"We do?" I asked.

"What do we need to choose between?" Lukas asked.

"You can both live here," Helen replied. "Menelaus and I will be very pleased if you wish to do that. So will Hermione and Leda. We hope you'll manage this olive grove. But if there's anything else you wish to do, you can do it."

"I wouldn't live here," I said, "without doing something useful for the kingdom."

"Neither would I," Lukas said. "I'd love working in this olive grove with Timon. I don't need another choice."

"But you have another choice," Helen said, "whether you want it or not."

"What's our other choice?" I asked.

Helen turned to me and laughed. Now I knew why she'd always looked at me the way she had. Whenever she saw me, she saw Paris as well.

"You could go to Italy," she said.

I scoffed. "Why would we go to Italy?"

Helen's Orphans

"You're a Trojan," Helen replied. "Our traders tell us the Trojans who survived the war made their way to Italy. They're building a city there. Menelaus and I recently had a conversation with one of our traders who travels to the city. She said the older people there tell a story they'd heard in Troy—Paris and Helen had a child. They naturally wonder what happened to the child. Is he dead? Is he alive? And if he's alive, where is he now?"

"The truth is about to come out," Lukas said, "no matter what we do."

Helen nodded. "That seems likely to happen."

"You haven't answered my question," I said. "Why would Lukas and I want to go to Italy? I have a Greek mother. I'm therefore Greek. Why wouldn't I want to live with her in Greece? And with my sister, grandmother and stepfather?"

Helen looked at me as if I were that thumb-sucking boy again. "You're a Trojan prince."

I shook my head. "I never asked to be a Trojan prince."

"Neither did your father," Helen said. "But you're more than that. You're the only surviving member of the Trojan royal family. We've learned your paternal grandparents, Priam and Hecuba, died on their way to Italy. You're their only living descendant."

"Tomorrow, when Timon turns eighteen," Lukas asked, "he'll be the king of the Trojans in Italy?"

Helen shrugged. "If they want a king. If Timon wants to be their king. Menelaus and I can ask our trader friend to be our ambassador to the Trojans in Italy. She can let them know the child Paris and I had in Troy is alive and well in Sparta."

"She shouldn't leave out," Lukas said, "he was raised and educated in an orphanage."

"In Helen's excellent orphanage," I said. "And with you by my side every step of my way to correct, guide and inspire me."

"True," Lukas said, laughing.

I turned to Helen. "You and Menelaus can send an ambassador to Italy and let the Trojans there know I'm alive and well in Sparta. But she should also inform them I won't pay them a visit anytime soon. That's because I want no part of being a prince or king. I'd much rather tend an olive grove and compose songs with Lukas in Greece."

I could tell by the looks on their faces neither Helen nor Lukas wished to oppose me on that.

Timon

"Does Leda know," I asked Helen, "I'm her grandson?"

"She's known that," Helen replied, "since the day I brought you back from Troy."

"Does Hermione know I'm her brother?"

"She knows."

"Does Orestes know I'm his cousin?"

"He knows. And he and Hermione are both at the palace now with Menelaus. They and Leda and I would very much like to share our evening meal with you and Lukas. It would just be the seven of us. We prepare our own meals. Menelaus and I decided when we married we wouldn't need personal servants. We found other jobs for those who were still working here then."

"I'm glad to know that," Lukas said. "Timon and I will help with the meals and any other work that needs to be done from now on. I have no wish to be idle."

"Nor do I," I said.

Timon

Helen, Lukas and I rose to our feet again.

Lukas turned to Helen. "Can we see the swans on our way to the palace?"

"We can do that," she replied. "And I wouldn't be surprised if we'll also find Leda at their pond now. She's especially looking forward to this evening at the palace. It'll be the first time she'll sit down to enjoy a meal with all of her grandchildren."

Timon

After we'd walked awhile in the new lives Helen's disclosures had created for all three of us, she turned to Lukas.

"Is your uncle your only remaining relative?" she asked.

"He is," Lukas replied.

Helen's Orphans

"I'd like to meet him," Helen said.

After we'd walked a bit further, Helen turned to Lukas again.

"Maybe," she said, "you and Timon should take a carriage and bring your uncle to the palace for a visit."

"We'll do that," Lukas said.

Timon

As we approached Leda and the swans, I turned to Helen. "What's the name of the city the Trojans are building in Italy?"

Helen looked at me and grinned. "You'd need to know that if you and Lukas ever decided to pay them a visit."

Lukas shrugged. "We could pay them a visit someday."

"Yes, you could," Helen said. "I understand they call their city Rome."

Made in the USA
Monee, IL
20 December 2020